Ric Couchman was born in Georgetown, Guyana. An average performer in high school, he grew interested in serious scholarship after he began undergraduate and graduate studies in Theology at the Jamaica Theological Seminary and at the Caribbean Graduate School of Theology. His love of poetry, prose, and drama evolved in high school, but it was during his educational experience at the tertiary level that he became serious about writing and that his literary appreciation and his love of philosophy emerged. Ric Couchman credits Mary Shelley, Soren Kierkegaard, Albert Camus, and Guyanese novelist Edgar Mittelholzer as the writers who have most influenced him. His passion for bushcraft and for independent living in the outdoors, his occupation as an educator at a New York City high school, his Caribbean upbringing, and his childhood exposure to Hinduism, Islam, Roman Catholicism, and Evangelical Christianity while growing up in Guyana all inform his writings and influence his unique voice and style.

ALSO BY RIC COUCHMAN

Musings from Outside the Universal

A Famine of Tears

Blueprint for a Nihilism

Conflagration of Ouranos

3:00 A.M.

Following the Blue Morpho

From Faith to Faith

THE LiTTLE BOY

FROM

WATER STREET

RIC COUCHMAN

A WAN WAN DUTTY BOOK

FOR

ROBERTO

IMANI

~~CARLOS~~

KARA

CAIO

"I read the instruction You gave in I Samuel 15: 3. Children and infants!??? What kind of Monster are You? How could you?"

                                                            --Anyone with a conscience

THE LITTLE BOY

FROM

WATER STREET

1

*A*nd just like that, little Hans Kindermann appeared. In a crib. In a small room. Before that moment he was non-being. He was without antecedent, as was also the room and everything in it. In that room, in that crib, there began his existence. Right there. Standing in a crib. Watching. He was not there. Then there he was. In a room, standing in a crib. Watching.

My existence began at exactly the moment of little Hans's beginning in that room. I, too, am without antecedent. I did not exist before that moment. I, too, simply appeared.

Who am I? I truly do not know. You can call me Eyes, for I feel like I am eyes only. I have no form. I am without mass. I have no eyes, yet I see. I see, even though I have no eyes. I am consciousness perhaps. Who knows? All I know is that I can see. However, I can see only events pertaining to little Hans. These events or existence moments are largely non-sequential, lacking contiguity and connection. They appear, for the most part, as vignettes, linked only by a kind of darkness. I watch these events without judgement. I watch Hans without judgement. I feel that which he feels, but I am unattached to his feelings.

There he is standing in the crib, always coming into being exactly as I see him now – standing in the crib. The crib stands flush against the wall of the small room. To the right of the crib is a twin-sized bed. He stands at the opposite rail of the crib gripping its top tightly with both hands and watching the scene before him. There is a hint of sadness in his eyes, not because of the scene before him but on account of his inner essence. The sadness in his eyes reflects his inner essence. "Inner essence" is a redundant phrase I suppose. Let's just say, the sadness in his eyes reflects his essence.

Our little boy sees a man and a woman in the room. They are across from the crib. He watches them. As he watches them, there is no emotion on his young face. That is not to say that he is merely a passive onlooker. There is a soft innocence there, and a mature curiosity, and a certain sadness.

The man is attending to the woman who is sobbing quietly. He gently cleans a gash on her right thumb. They are both sitting on the wooden floor. Before them lies a small basin of water now rendered crimson by the woman's blood.

As the man cleans the wound, the little child observes the tenderness and care with which the act is performed and contrasts the caring tenderness of that moment with the angry violence that immediately preceded it. He did not directly witness the violence; he intuits it. I, too, can sense it. I can feel it. The violence has left its odorous presence in that small room. Its smell hangs heavily in the room, like the dust cloud from the aftermath of a volcanic eruption.

And such is the little boy's paradoxical welcome into his world. So begins his existence as he is inserted between a moment of violence and a moment of tenderness.

The scene before me is gradually fading. The little boy continues watching from his standing position in the crib. He watches the man and the woman without judgement. He watches them, trying to make sense of this improbable juxtaposition of violence and tenderness, trying to understand. Then everything completely fades to black.

2

*B*efore I continue, let me state clearly: The little boy cannot tell his story. He has no one to whom he could speak, and what also makes it difficult is that he lives in timeless moments or pockets of existence. His existence is always past and present and future. It happened, it is happening, it will happen. Telling his story is only possible because it can be observed, and since I am the only one who can observe it, I am the only one who can tell it. His existence is the predicate of my existence, and because of that I must tell his story. In that way I am the medium through whom his existence becomes apprehended by others.

The little boy's world has expanded, but not by much. He stands just outside a house. The house is there, but there is no clarity to it. A few trees, a cloudless sky, and other houses seem an apparent part of the background but more on account of intuition than sight. Even the little boy himself appears vague, like a figure coming out of the shadows. He holds a dark-blue toy revolver which seems bigger than the little hand holding it. The toy gun is in sharp focus, contrasting strongly with the blurred, black, and white image of the boy and his surroundings, like the effects of a wide-open aperture upon a photographic composition, blurring everything in the background and sharpening the blue-accented toy gun in the foreground.

The little boy turns his attention to a pile of shrimps lying on an old zinc sheet beside the short stair to his apartment. I have no idea about the size of the apartment because it is out of focus. The boy places the toy gun on one of the steps, picks up one of the shrimps between the thumb and forefinger of his right hand, and puts it in his mouth. Moments later, his face contorts, and he spits the chewed-up shrimp on the ground, retching but bringing up nothing. And then everything becomes black again and the little boy is no longer there.

When did these moments of existence take place? I cannot provide you an answer. They are timeless as the boy is timeless. They are always happening, always beginning, unfolding, and ending, and always in the parentheses of blackness, disappearing then recurring, disappearing and recurring, but only I can see them. Do you get it? Does that make sense to you? I do not know how best to explain it. I am limited in how best I can explain the phenomenon on account of the limits of language.

And so the boy is always a little boy, with variations in his age, his appearance, and his immediate surroundings, with each existence event repeated, not compiled together all in one breath but randomly and individually, and never in the same sequence. Each existence moment is complete in itself and independent of the other existent moments, and yet, together they sum up the little boy's being. They sum up his essence. However, these existence moments mean nothing without my perception of them. In fact, I do not know if they exist outside of my perception of them or whether the little child is apart from my perception of him. And, I am aware of my own being only in my perception of him. Without him I do not exist, and yet I am independent of him. I warrant that any speculation as to who I am would be futile. I suggest that you waste no time on that pursuit.

The Little Boy From Water Street

3

*C*aution. The existence event now unfolding before me might cause much alarm. The little boy, looking more like a toddler, is sitting cross-legged on the ground just outside a dark-grey apartment. The image is quite vivid. The apartment is on the lower level of a two-storey building with three apartments, two on the lower level and one on the upper. The building is raised a few feet off the ground so that one could easily crawl under it. The child is shirtless and appears to be wearing a dingy, cloth diaper. The front of the apartment is enclosed by a hastily put together wooden fence roughly about six feet high, with palings of varying lengths and width. Above the little child, perched on a small wooden structure extending from the rafters, is a squirrel monkey, one of the smaller species of primates. A small chain attached to a leather buckle around its slender waist restricts its movement beyond about five feet.

On the ground just in front of the little child lies a litter of about four recently born kittens. Above, the squirrel monkey moves raucously back and forth, occasionally expelling fecal matter on the ground not too far from the child below. To the squirrel monkey's fecal deposits, the child pays no mind. He intently focuses on the litter of kittens. Their eyes are barely open. In his right hand, the little boy holds a not-so-heavy, grey, wooden clothes beater - a device in shape of a paddle used in doing laundry by hand.

The image quickly changes. The little boy repeatedly strikes the kittens with the clothes beater. The force of the blows is from that of a small child but, nonetheless, lethal. In the aftermath of that battering, the little boy seems unmoved. He stares down at the furry sight before him, watching them with his large, sad eyes, curious, just curious.

And there the existence event, the taking of the lives of four little kittens, the killing of four little kittens, ends, fading to black until repeated again in my perception, whenever.

I have seen that existence event many times previously. Call it what you like. Mindless. Cruel. If you expect from me any emotional response, my reply to you is that it is not my place to feel. You might recall I said I am eyes only. I am perception, the mere custodian of the little boy's existence moments. It might be your place, perhaps, to judge or to feel some emotion or the other; it is not mine... Wait! Hang on a minute. I see another image taking shape.

Several children sit on a pew in a small church. The little boy, now older then he appears in the preceding existence event, sits among them. They are learning the Catechism pursuant to their participating in the rite of the second of the three Sacraments of Initiation.

A woman stands in front of the children, guiding them as they eagerly recite the ten Commandments. I hear the little boy quite distinctly; his voice stands out from the rest:

"...*Remember the Sabbath day to keep it holy. Honor they father and thy mother. Thou shalt not kill. Thou...*"

The image gradually fades into the background, leaving only the darkness. And from the darkness the voices, eager and innocent, as though caught in a loop, waft forth, "*Thou shalt not kill. Thou shalt not kill...Thou shalt not...*"

4

A two-storey building presents itself. Two apartments on the lower floor and the entire upper floor occupied by a family of about seven - a mother, a father, and five daughters. The little boy is with the five sisters on that upper floor. It appears that the little boy's mother has arranged for her upstairs neighbors to babysit him while she is away on some errand. I cannot describe the flat. Everything is a dark blur except for the girls (all teenagers) and the little boy whom I can see clearly. The girls giggle as they surround the little boy. He looks scared. The girls undress him and take turns unwantedly touching his boyhood. The little boy pulls away. The girls persist, still giggling. The little boy feels trapped. He pleads with them to stop. The girls persist, still giggling. The little boy continues to plead with them to stop, the tears streaming down his face. He does not understand what is happening. He is afraid, confused. He continues to plead with them to stop, plaintively begging them to stop, and in between his pleas, wondering why.

Another image takes shape. The oldest of the teenage girls lies supine, her legs spread apart. The other four girls grab the boy and position him not too gently on top of their sister. The sisters are all giggling. The little boy screams. He does not understand what is happening or why it is happening. His very inner screams out. He is revulsed by the happening, at being "*so rudely forced.*"

Somehow, the image imprinted in the little boy's memory is imprinted in my consciousness as well. I see the things that he remembers and sees even though I haven't seen them. The image of the naked teenage girls stayed with him, as well as an image that looked like a fish's gill with nappy, black hair around it. That latter image never left the little boy, and that image has somehow been transferred to me; it has never left me.

At this point the existence moment encapsulating that violent episode ends, to be relived again and again in memory, but never revealed in speech or tapestry.

5

*H*ans sits at the table looking down at the area on his inside upper right thigh. He is screaming in pain – my first perception of his feeling of pain, and his first memory of pain. He had just knocked over his enamel cup of Red Rose tea, the scorching hot liquid easily making its way through his striped, red pajama pants and narrowly missing his genitals. The man (now with a beard and a serious looking face) and the pregnant woman sitting at the table both get up from their chairs and rush to the little boy's side. The man remarks about how clumsy the little boy is, his face a picture of dissatisfaction. The woman takes off his pajama pants and examines the burned area (exposing the patch of raw flesh on his inside upper right thigh), a look of concern on her face.

The apartment is a small, two-room space with a bedroom and dining/living. A tiny kitchen, accessible only from the outside, is attached to the side of the apartment. The little boy's world is gradually expanding, moving beyond the confines of rooms.

Allow me to make the following clarification: My objective is not to entertain you with an on-the-edge-of-your-seat story of Hans following the usual linear, beginning-middle-end model that terminates on some climax and resolves some human problem. Look elsewhere for the didactic template and imperatives for storytelling as laid out in *Poetics* by "the Master of those who know," namely, plot driven by any of the four basic levels of conflict, manipulating the passage of time through narration, action, and dialogue, the resolution of conflict, character development, and more. Look elsewhere for prognoses, themes, or philosophical viewpoints. If you come across any of these here, their presence is certainly not by design. I give you only that which I see, the little boy's existence moments as they appear to me, following which you may feel free to do your own analysis and arrive at your own conclusions. I got carried away there for a bit. Why don't I just shut up and get on with the task at hand?

6

*I*t is the night before Christmas. Isn't that how Clement Moore's classic Christmas poem begins? The little boy is in the same two-room apartment with the man and the pregnant woman. They sit in the neat but sparsely furnished living/dining room. The little boy, now slightly bigger than the little child we first met in the crib, is excitedly expectant. Father Christmas is supposed to be bringing him toys, and he hopes to find them tomorrow on the small dining table. But as far as the little boy is concerned there is a problem - a problem that he is afraid to articulate or to bring up with the man and the woman.

How is Father Christmas going to gain access into the apartment? The apartment has no chimney. As far as the little boy knows, chimneys do not exist in his part of the world. And not only does the apartment have no chimney, but the only door to the apartment along with its two windows are all secured from the inside by metal bolts. This realization worries the little boy, for if Father Christmas has no access to the apartment that means no toys for him for Christmas. The little boy grows increasingly worried.

You might notice that the little boy's existence events I present have no dialogue, meaningful ones that is. His world is a muted world - for the most part void of conversation, void of speech, void of verbal engagement. It is a silent world. The man does not speak with him. The woman does not speak with him. If they do speak, they speak to him, not with him.

So what is a child to do in a silent world, in a world in which she is expected to be seen but not heard? She creates her own world. He populates his world with people from his own imagination. She gives them their own dialogue. He creates substitutes for the elements lacking in his world. But I digress. I must remember that my purpose is not to present analysis but to unseal the little boy's moments of existence.

It is Christmas morning. The boy sits at the table examining his cowboy toy gun and holster. He beams with excitement over his Christmas presents but is puzzled as to how Father Christmas gained entrance into the apartment. The only explanation he could think of was that Father Christmas apparently possesses the power to pass through solid surfaces just like the man does.

Yes indeed. It seems obvious to the little boy that the man is endowed with power to pass through walls, for how else could he account for seeing him lying fast asleep in bed beside the pregnant woman when he wakes up in the morning? The man always left the apartment in late afternoon wearing his black beret and dressed in his khaki shirt and pants. The woman and the little boy would retire to sleep just after nightfall, and behold, the next morning the man would be lying in bed beside the woman. How could that be possible? How could the man get into the apartment with the door and all the windows firmly bolted from the inside while both the boy and the woman lay fast asleep? The little boy could only conclude that the man had special powers which made him able to get into the apartment whenever it was securely bolted from the inside. And now it appears that Father Christmas has similar power in the absence of a chimney from which to climb down into the apartment.

But the intriguing question of how Father Christmas could possibly have gained entry into the chimney-less apartment quickly gives place to curiosity when a stranger (introduced to the little boy as Grandfather) suddenly shows up at the door that Christmas morning

Mr. Grandfather appears to be closely connected to the man. However, they hardly speak with each other during his visit. When they do speak, their exchange seems labored. They look uncomfortable in each other's presence.

The little boy is awed by the visitor, a giant of a man, tall, sturdily built, of dark-brown complexion, and with black, curly hair. The scene emphatically and suddenly shifts to the outdoors. As to which part of the outdoors, I cannot say. The backdrop has the fuzziness of a Van Gogh.

Mr. Grandfather places his hands under the little boy's armpits, picks him up from off the ground, and, extending his arms upwards, holds him aloft, his legs dangling in the air. Then Mr. Grandfather deftly turns the little boy around in mid-air and seats him behind his neck on his broad shoulders. Just listen to the little boy as he giggles and screams with delight. I have no other existence event in my custody of any such joyous engagement between him and any other adult.

7

The pregnant woman and the man are not in the apartment. The little boy is there alone. He stands facing the only window in the room - the bedroom. Only the boy and the window are in focus. Everything else is blurred, out of focus. There is nothing else visible in the room.

The window is open. It is one of those wooden windows that swings in and out. A floral, cloth blind stretches across the bottom half of the window, providing some privacy from peering eyes outside. The light from the sun makes its way through the cloth blind, illuminating the little boy's face.

The little boy's head reaches just past the level of the windowsill. In his hand is a small matchbox with some matches in it. What do you expect a little boy to do if he is left all alone at home with the door to the apartment padlocked from the outside. He might play with matches - the same matches he sees the man use when lighting his cigarettes, the same matches he sees the woman use when she lights the kerosene stove or the kerosene lamp, the same matches he sees the man and woman use when they burn garbage on the rubbish heap in the backyard. And when they are not at home and he is left alone, one of the things he does is play with matches.

The little boy reaches into the matchbox (a red matchbox with a lighthouse on it), takes out a match, lights it, watches it burst into flames, then blows it out. He lights another match, but this time he holds the lit match to the cloth screen. The morning sun envelops the cloth screen in its soft sunlight. The little boy continues to hold the lit match close to the screen. He blows out the match as soon as it burns close to his thumb, then stands staring at the translucently bright, sun-lit screen.

As he stands watching the screen, the little boy notices the two outer parts of the screen slowly changing from brown to black. Then he sees a flame appear, and in that instant, he realizes that the cloth screen had caught fire. He hadn't noticed it at first on account of the screen's immersion in the sunlight. His large, brown eyes wide and welling up with tears, and terror and panic filling his innocent face, the little boy stands before the blazing screen transfixed when, suddenly, a huge splash of water comes flying out of a bucket and through the window from the outside, dousing the flame-engulfed cloth screen. A neighbor who had been drawing water from the standpipe just outside the window had seen the cloth screen on fire and immediately took action to contain it.

Everything fades after that moment. All I see following is blackness. But from the darkness I hear voices. I cannot see, but I can hear. I hear the man's loud voice and the pleading, tremulous voice of the little boy. I cannot make out what is being said, but from the tone and loudness of the man's voice one could infer that he is very angry.

After a brief pause, a loud snap breaks the silence. A piercing scream immediately breaks forth out of the dark foreground. And then another snap, and another, and another, and more screams, the little boy's screams. One cannot begin to imagine the fear, the pain, the confusion, and the violence emanating out of that blacked out moment of existence.

8

Something doesn't feel right. Something is brewing. There is something ominous going on beyond the little boy's world. There is tension in the air. The little boy can feel it. He remembers the short, fat white men he saw in their khaki uniforms, with their large heads, and their huge helmets, and their guns - scary looking white soldiers in their short, khaki pants, tall socks, and black boots. He remembers seeing them in trucks driving in a convoy along the public road. He had never seen white people before. He had seen them only in movies and in comic books. He wishes his eyes were as blue as theirs, his skin as light as theirs, and his hair of the same texture as theirs. He does not like his nappy hair. It is always difficult to comb, and it always hurts whenever he tries to comb it. He also likes the way white people speak and tries to imitate their manner of speaking. He thinks they speak better than the way people on Water Street speak. But again I digress…

The little boy has heard talk of riots. He has heard talks among some of the neighbors of the man's having a gun hidden in the apartment. He has heard talk of police officers searching the man's apartment for the firearm. Just vague talk, with no clear image of anyone speaking of the things of which he hears. All this talk excites the little boy. A gun in the apartment? That excites him even more. He thinks adventure. He seriously considers looking for the firearm. Imagine that. The man has a real gun. The man must be someone special. The little boy feels proud that the man has a gun. He cannot wait to tell his friends.

The little boy is alone again in the bedroom. On this occasion only a small corner of the room is in focus. A tall cupboard stands off to the side. The little boy stands in front of the cupboard, looking up. He climbs up on a chair or on the edge of a bed in the room. I can't quite make out which, but he climbs up on something to make it easy for him to reach the top of the cupboard. He passes his right hand across the top of the cupboard expecting to find the gun. Nothing. No gun. But his hand touches something. He retrieves it. A glass jar with a thick roll of blue, Malali twenty-dollar bills. His heart racing, the little boy unrolls the roll of twenty-dollar bills, takes one of them, puts the rest of the bills back into the glass jar, and returns the jar back to its place. He hopes the man does not miss the twenty-dollar bill he now has in his pants pocket. He worries that the man would find out about the missing money; he worries that the man will know that he took the money (for, after all, the man knows all things) and that the result will be more red welts from the vicious application of the man's leather waist-belt on his back. But for the little boy, desire, as well as the excitement from taking the risk were stronger than the anticipation of receiving painful retribution from the man for stealing the money. What does he plan to do with the twenty? He has no idea. He certainly couldn't spend it, for little children do not go around spending twenty-dollar bills in the village shops unless they have a written note from a parent. Just spending a ten-cent bit would raise suspicion and even more so a Malali. A shopkeeper would not allow any purchase but would confiscate the money and immediately alert the man or the woman.

9

*V*eronica's passion is cinema - the arena of film, the moving image. It is after midnight, and she and the little boy have just left Mr. Deodat's cinema. Two films were shown that night. One of them about a woman with snakes in her head. The little boy is scared. As I said, the woman's passion is losing herself in a film. She is happiest whenever she is in the cinema. It doesn't matter what genre the film, just being in the cinema is everything to her. She always takes the little boy along with her. The experience of the moving image on screen, and the experience of cinema are her lasting gifts to him. He, too, gets lost in the on-screen experience. Mr. Deodat's cinema is his *Cinema Paradiso*.

Tonight's film, "The Gorgon", scared the bejesus out of him, but he will be more than ready to return to watch another horror film with the woman again. But it is not the film that is the scarier part of this night or of other nights after leaving the cinema. It is the anticipation of walking along the dark public road and having to pass the old Chinese cemetery on the way home and afterwards having to walk through a very dark alley before turning the corner on to Water Street.

As on all the other nights when returning from the cinema, the woman tells the little boy to walk in front of her. As also on those other nights he is shivering with fear. He hesitates as they near the cemetery. The woman urges him on, annoyed at his lingering. The little boy pouts and continues hesitantly past the cemetery. And in his usual thinking regarding the woman's habit of making him walk in front of her, he concludes that she was herself too scared to walk in front of him because of her own fear of jumbies or duppies and that she was only too willing to selfishly sacrifice him to save herself, in which case those creatures from the dead would get to him first, giving her the opportunity to turn and run away from the danger. He does not believe that is fair at all.

The little boy and the woman pass the cemetery without incident. He is visibly relieved, but there is still the dark alleyway to negotiate and the jumbies that prowl there with whom they still must contend.

They arrive at the dark alleyway, and the little boy stops, expecting the woman to hold his hand or to have him walk behind her...."For that is what a good mother is supposed to do, right?" Such was his thought. Yes, I do hear his thoughts sometimes. But instead of holding his hand as he expects, the woman yells at him, telling him to keep on walking ahead of her. He walks along the dark alley, looking back every few steps to make sure the woman is still behind him. She is there, but to the little boy's surprise she does not look scared. In fact, she never looks scared, but the little boy is not buying it; in his mind she is simply pretending not to be scared.

Hans wants to cry as he always has all those other times, but he is too focused on the possible appearance of jumbies to shed tears now. He grows angry at the woman for putting his life at risk by having him walk in front of her and hopes that she would never take him with her to the cinema again.

To the little boy's relief, they make it safely through the dark alley. He puts out of his mind any thought of not wanting to go again to the cinema with the woman. He cannot wait to go again, horror film, or cemetery, or dark alleyway or whatever.

10

I really do not know who I am or from whence I am. I have no form, no body, yet I see. All around me is darkness, thick darkness. I am aware of the darkness in front of me and on either side of me but not behind me. I assume that it is dark there too. In fact, I cannot look behind me, nor can I look to my left or right. Such actions require a head to turn or a body to move, and I have no body. My orientation is always frontal, and the only things I see are the little boy's event images, his existence moments. When those images are gone, I too am gone. I "am" only when I "see" (or hear) or "perceive" those images. Those images and I are linked, but only in as far as I behold them. I observe them, and that is all. And I observe without attachment - without desire or aversion or judgement. The little boy and I are linked just as much as his existence moments and I are linked. And just as I exist because he is, he exists (well, in the images) because I am. I do not like or dislike that which I see. I simply see without investment or without commitment. I watch without feelings.

The little boy's world expands beyond the apartment and incorporates other space and objects. Off to the side of the apartment is a huge open vat filled with rainwater. Just behind the vat is a house on stilts - the apartment owner's house. The little boy stands beside the vat with a cat in his arms - one of the usual stray cats about the yard. The feline attempts to extricate itself from his arms but without success.

A sewing pin protrudes from between the little boy's lips. He sticks the pin into the writhing cat's side and throws it quickly into the water-filled vat. Submerged very briefly, the cat swims to the opposite side of the vat and jumps out of it to safety. One fewer life left, he muses, as he watches the cat scamper off. He stands at just about above average height for a little boy, with matte bronze skin and a medium-sized clump of nappy hair on his head. Shirtless, and no shoes on his feet, he wears only a pair of dingy, khaki pants torn on both sides of his behind and exposing his butt cheeks.

11

*H*ans stands bare-feet beside a standpipe filling a white plastic bucket with water, his only attire - a dingy, torn-up pair of short, batty pants. His chest heaves as if he is struggling to breathe. He takes intermittent short breaths as tears stream down his face, mingling with the clear watery snot slowly making its way down his nostrils. He turns off the standpipe's faucet, picks up the bucket filled with water, and turns to head up the short stairs to the apartment. His frail, bronze back reveals several fresh welts from the leather waist-belt.

*O*n the kitchen table lies a book, the man's book. The little boy sees it, walks up to the table, pulls out a chair, sits down, and opens the book. He turns the pages and is surprised to see that it is without pictures. A book without pictures!? He is incredulous. He looks at the book's title. On the cover it reads, *The Republic of Plato*. He reads the title out loud (vocalizing the last word as "plateau," with a long "a"), then begins to read the book, or tries to read it, surmising that it must be a book of tremendous significance since it belongs to the man. He attempts to read a few paragraphs. The words make no sense to him, but he feels a sense of pride and accomplishment at his reading the man's book.

At this point the image changes, presenting me with another image. Again the little boy is passing by the kitchen table and again notices a book lying on top of it, another of the man's books. Curious, he stops at the table, picks up the book, and turns a few pages. A quotation on the page following the table of contents page struck him: "...for, not to desire or admire, if a man could learn it, were more than to walk all day like a Sultan of old in a garden of spice." The little boy reads it out loud several times, intuiting a sense of the quotation's profundity but unable to understand its meaning. He puts the book back in its place, continues his way, and resolves to pursue the quotation's meaning.

13

The image, or scene, or vignette set before me is not unlike the others I have previously shared with you. They are of various degrees of composition. Some are more exposed than others, some more vivid than others, some more detailed, some less detailed or having no image at all but replaced by only darkness, and some distorted. The one thing they all have in common is that they appear to me only in black, grey, or white. The toy gun in accented blue is the only exception – a rather strange phenomenon.

In the image currently before me, the woman appears as if illuminated by a spotlight. Her affect is somber, distant, as if she is lost in thought, her mind someplace else. The vague figure of the little boy shows up beside her, holding what seems to be a container filled with wooden clothes-pins.

The woman bends over, picks up an item of clothing from a large basin on the ground, accepts two pins from the little boy, and fastens them to the item of clothing she placed on the line.

The little boy notices her swollen left eye, a black ring encircling it, like the black eye he has seen in comic books. He stares at the black eye in amazement. He had never seen a real black eye before. All he thinks of is how the woman's black eye looks exactly like the ones he has seen in comic books.

The woman had introduced the little boy to comic books, opening a rich new world for him, stimulating his imagination, and helping him develop his reading skills. He read all genres – cartoon comics, Marvel superheroes comics, western comics, war comics, and fairy tale comics. Eventually, the woman gave him full responsibility for borrowing books for her from Cyril's Comic Book Library; her favorite genre was romance. Unfortunately, Mr. Cyril caught him stealing and hiding books down his pants on a few occasions, resulting in his eventual ban from the library.

Now regarding the woman's black eye, it never crosses the little boy's mind to wonder regarding its origin.

14

On one of the walls in the living room of the apartment hang three framed portraits - one of the Sacred Heart of Jesus, the second of a bearded man in black beret, and the third, of another bearded man also in black beret. The word, "Venceremos," is written on a sign that hangs under the portraits. The man in the third portrait has long, black hair flowing from under his beret down to his neck. He appears the most intriguing of the three, at least in the little boy's mind. This morning, he passes by the portraits, and as he has done on all the other occasions when walking by them, he casts his eyes across the portraits, his eyes lingering on the one the man identified as Che. The little boy has always been fascinated by the portrait of Jesus, with his blonde hair and soft blue eyes, but it is the face in that third portrait that always stirs him. There is something about that faraway, melancholy, and decisive look, as if he were looking into the future. That the two bearded men in black berets shared a spot on the wall with gentle Jesus was, for the little boy, simply incredible. That means they must be men of extraordinary importance.

But Gentle Jesus confuses the heck out of him. He cannot reconcile his seeming docility and his gentleness with his apparent willingness to consign to hell those people who do not believe in him. Wasn't that what Pastor Brimstone said during one of his open-air crusades - that people who do not believe in Jesus will be damned in hellfire? Everywhere the little boy turns, someone is always preaching that message - on the radio, by the roadside, in Sunday School. The fires of hell shadow him. And even though he believes, he still feels he is going to hell. Hardly a day passes without that thought making its appearance in his mind. Now that's exactly the reason he ran out of Mr. Deodat's cinema in fear and trembling on Easter Monday as he was watching a Jesus movie, *The Greatest Story Ever Told*, during a school matinee. In his view, there is nothing great about the Jesus story if he will be consigned to hell.

15

"You piece of shit!" Did you hear that? Forgive me. I forgot. You cannot hear it; only I can hear it. But if you could hear it, you would surely not miss the loathing and the disdain in those words. Those are the man's words, directed at the little boy. I do not see either of them, but I know they are there in the darkness that lies behind the thick, grey fog.

A long silence follows, then several familiar snaps of the leather waist-belt on flesh. Screams. Silence. And the thick, grey fog dissipates, leaving behind the darkness.

16

*I*magine you are a dragonfly. The day is bright and sunny, and you have just made short work of a hapless insect that happened across your path. You devour it in short order, and now you are looking for a nice, shady area on which to land and to cool your wings. Overheating is very uncomfortable among your kind. You see a paling fence with a tall, jamoon tree towering over it and providing lots of shade. You see a little boy draped lazily along one of its branches. You pay him no mind and make a perfect landing on one of the palings. Since time is not a thing among your kind, you have no idea of the length of time you spent cooling down.

You feel that you have cooled down considerably, and so you prepare to get airborne again. Before you can take flight, you feel a vicelike grip on your left wing. You recognize the little boy; he stands behind you. He lifts you off the fence, holding your wing between his thumb and forefinger then takes the right wing and brings both your wings together behind you. You can feel the delicate structure of your translucent wings becoming compromised on account of the vicelike grip.

The next thing you know is that you are being lowered by your segmented abdomen (you might refer to it as a tail) into the opening of an ant nest, with your two wings secured to the ground behind you. Your segmented abdomen is positioned full length in the hole, and your wings are fastened to the ground by a mud paste. Escape is impossible.

Why is this happening? Why is the little boy doing this to you? You have no idea. Soon you feel the sensation of many things crawling up your tail (segmented abdomen) and along your thorax, and finally over your bulging, compound eyes. But far worse than the crawling sensation is the unbearable sting and pain you feel from the mandibles of those crawling things. The pain is more than you can bear, and you soon lose consciousness and are no more.

17

The little boy watches the scene before him. He refuses to believe that which he sees. The woman is in a rage. Before her is the leather grip - the grip containing all the man's photographs, his coins, memorabilia, and other mementoes from his world travels as a mariner. The little boy always looked forward to those rare occasions on which the man opened the grip to organize the items therein. In fascination, he would stand beside the man watching. There was something special about viewing the items contained in that grip. It allowed the little boy's imagination to take flight. But now the unthinkable is unfolding before his very eyes. Heartbroken, he watches as the woman sits on the floor before the open grip and rips to shreds all the man's photographs and scatters them in every direction around her.

The man enters the room and stands frozen in place, aghast at the sight before him. He has a beard now, like the three men on the wall. The little boy watches him intently, observing as the man's customary narrowing of the eyes, firm setting of the jaw, pursed lips, and hardening facial features give place to a look of disbelief and then anguish .

Letting out an agonizing cry, the man rushes towards the open grip on the floor, falls on his knees before it, and weeps inconsolably. The woman gets up from her seated position on the floor and walks away out of the apartment. The little boy watches quietly, curiously wondering at the man's profound sadness, seeing him at his most vulnerable and in tears. Their eyes meet, but briefly, for the man quickly averts his eyes. His humiliation is clear. His shame is obvious. The little boy had never seen the man cry before, had never seen any man cry before, and that confused him. It made him uncomfortable.

18

I see the little boy sitting on the ground. He is talking to himself, but I cannot hear what he is saying. He is looking down at an insect. Its two wings are positioned together behind it and are secured to the ground by a mud paste. Its tail seems to be partially in a hole. The small hole in the ground before him appears to be the entrance and exit of an ants' nest. A clearly marked out pathway (presumably constructed by the little boy) leads to and from the nest which is decorated with a tiny paper flag (also crafted by the little boy). The insect, which looks like a dragonfly, is motionless. A train of ants is moving up and down its body while a long line streams its way to and from some other point on the ground.

The little boy continues talking to himself. Then he gets up, leaves, and returns a little later with a small container in his hand. He proceeds to pour some of the contents of the container onto the ants' nest. He watches as the ants scatter in a frenzy, their already short lifespan brought to an abrupt end by the liquid poured upon them.

Suddenly, the heavens unload a torrent of rain. Unmoved, the little boy raises his face, offering it to the cool raindrops. Rainstorm is weeping, he thinks to himself, remembering the story he heard in school of the indigenous girl who did not make it to the heavens in time because her broom, which she refused to leave behind, got stuck between the rain clouds.

Filled with delight, the little boy starts to jump up and down, laughing and giggling, as Rainstorm's tears soothe the welts and bruises on his exposed back.

I know what you are thinking. Actually,... scratch that; I do not know what you are thinking. I do, however, have a few questions. Have you already labeled and defined Hans from the few fuzzy images I have shown you, prognosticating his future based on the "studies" you might have heard about or read? Have you already written him off? Nah…no sarcasm in my questions, nor am I being combative. Honest. Just curious is all.

19

The rat-faced boy, that's how the little boy thinks of him - the older boy who punches him every time he sees him, every time their paths cross, and without cause, for absolutely no reason. The rat-faced boy named Stefan. Stefan, the altar boy who, while cleaning up after Mass, puts the holy chalice to his mouth and drains the residue of wine from it. The little boy, also an altar boy, has seen him with his very eyes.

He had just left the Chine'e shop after buying two loose cigarettes for the man. As he turns from the alley on to Water Street, he sees rat-faced Stefan approaching. Anticipating what is going to happen next and to avoid receiving the blow on his face or chest, the little boy turns sideways to absorb the impact on his upper left arm. Stefan punches him hard on his upper left arm and continued on his way, laughing. This has been the pattern for several weeks. The little boy lives in fear of these encounters.

Like a punching bag...that's what he feels like - beaten up by Stephan the bully, beaten by the man. Even the woman beats him. In fact, her beatings seem far more unbearable than the man's. Yet he bears her no malice. As with the man, he recalls receiving no tenderness from the woman. No hugs. No playful interaction. No moments of endearment. But despite the absence of these things, he reveres her. He considers her sacred. He desires her. No,... not in the manner you might think. Not in the manner the man desires her, culminating in the activity behind the dividing sheet, an activity incomprehensible to him and evoking in him an equally incomprehensible feeling. Not in the manner other men in the village desire her, like Mr. Mcrae, or Mr. Brummel, or Mr. Clamence, or Mr. Bromley, and others. No. His desire is not of the lusty, adult sort; his desire for her is child-like, innocent, pure, protective. He admires her, adores her, considers her beautiful, and she is indeed beautiful. She is his Jocasta, his desire, but his desire is that of a little child.

20

With rapt attention, the little boy listens as pandit Rabindranaut Sashtri tells the story of Arjuna. The great warrior stands in the chariot with Krishna, contemplating the latter's instructions. Krishna instructs him to kill his cousins in battle. This is another of those days when the little boy would show up at the Hindu temple looking for the pandit and hoping for another good story from the *Mahabharata*. The pandit tells him of Arjuna's refusal to kill his relatives and Krishna's explanation that his killing his evil cousins was his duty and that though he might destroy their bodies, he could never destroy their souls. The story reminds the little boy of a similar story he had heard in Sunday school. In that story, the one from the Bible, God instructs Abraham to kill his only son Yitzhak as some kind of test of his faith. The little boy thought that was a horrible thing for God to ask a father to do. When he said as much to Miss Apola Jist, his Sunday school teacher, Miss Jist explained that God was good and that He would never cause harm to come to a child. He was only testing Yitzhak's father

The little boy loves the Mahabharata stories more than the stories in the Holy Bible. For him the Bible stories come across as too serious. As for the Koran, it doesn't really have a lot of stories in it, just boring talk. Allah, the God of the Holy Koran, and Yahweh, the God of the Holy Bible, scare the hell out of him, especially Yahweh who seems to endorse the slaughter of children and women. He heard Pastor Brimstone reading that from somewhere in the Holy Bible. He could not believe it when he heard it.

In the Mahabharata though, the stories are far more exciting and entertaining. The gods of the Mahabharata do not generate fear in him as do the other two. They present as vibrant and energetic and seem almost human, whereas the other two take things too seriously. They remind the little boy of the morose and depressive looking icons in the cathedral. Even Father Teufel, the priest of the village Church at which he serves as an altar boy, always looks holy and sad and bored. On top of that, Easter is mostly about the terrible crucifixion of Jesus, with the possibility of going to Hell always hovering over you. On the other hand, the holidays of the religion of the Mahabharata are, for the little boy, super exciting. He loves Pagwah. The fun part of that holiday is engaging in water fights with his friends in the morning and in the afternoon sprinkling white powder and liquid red dye on each other.

And then there is Holi, with all the tiny clay lamps arranged on the steps of the houses on Water Street. The little boy would usually steal a few from his Hindu neighbors so that he could put them on the steps of his own apartment and affirm his participation in the festival of lights.

The one thing about his experience in Islam that he immensely enjoyed was learning Arabic and learning to read the Holy Koran. The man had asked the local imam to take him under his wings, which the imam did with much delight. The little boy enjoyed attending Maktab and learning to recite the Holy Koran. However, he was forced to stop after rat-faced Stefan and a few other boys kept teasing him and pulling at his clothing whenever they saw him heading to the mosque.

21

*P*eter's Hall Dispensary. So reads the sign in bold letters on the side of the building. The dispensary serves the health needs of the village inhabitants. Those seeking health care are mostly women and children.

The woman sits on a bench. The little boy leans against a wall beside her. He prefers to stand. They wait their turn to be called, having already checked in with the nurse at the triage station. The little boy appears to be in much discomfort and is favoring his upper left arm. A closer look reveals that the arm is swollen and inflamed. The little boy contorts his face on account of the pain.

Moments later, he is sitting in a room with a doctor who decides to lance the infected area of the arm to drain it of the buildup of pus.

22

He is kneeling in the confession booth, little Hans. I can barely make him out in the dark booth. He feels embarrassed about telling Father Teufel the bad things he has done, feeling certain that the priest will recognize him.

He begins, "Bless me, Father, for I have sinned. I can't remember how many confessions I have made to this point. Yesterday I lied to my father. I also stole milk powder from the pantry and two comic books from Cyril's comic book library."

Father Teufel, sitting on the other side of the booth, absolves the little boy of his sins and instructs him to recite a few "Hail Marys" as penance. He leaves the confessional energized and buoyant, relieved that at least for the time being his journey to limbo or purgatory or hell has been put on hold.

23

*T*he uncomfortable feeling of the needle piercing his gum as he sits in the dental chair. The sharp smell of the dental office. His first visit to a dentist. The dentist in his white lab coat. The man, standing off to the side, eyes narrow, lips pursed, jaw firmly set, facial features hardened, just watching. The little boy's mouth wide open. The numbing sensation around the area where his broken front tooth is, the remaining half still strong and immovable and permanent.

The dentist stands over him, in his hand a pair of dental pliers, the remaining half of the little boy's broken front tooth secure between its vice-like pincers. His little hands tightly grip the handles on either side of the chair, his entire body wound up, tense, rigid. He hears the dentist breathing heavily. The dentist pulls, and pulls, and pulls, then rocks the tooth back and forth, back, and forth, but the immovable half-tooth remains unmoved. And all the while the little boy experiences unimaginable pain, his knuckles white from gripping the sides of the chair, the local anesthesia powerless to numb the pain.

The tooth is finally pulled, plucked out. Left in its place is unbearable pain. Darkness replaces the scene, but the two perpetrators of the violence in that room are still there in the darkness. All is now silent except for faint, whimpering sounds.

The pain is still there. It never left. It merely left its residency in the physical domain of the little boy's mouth and body, taking up, instead, permanent residency in his consciousness, in his very soul, deep inside his soul. He never wants to see another dentist again, ever, or to have his teeth examined again, ever.

And now another image. The little boy now has a tooth in place of the extracted one, a partial denture with a single tooth, the kind toothless old people wear in their mouths. He now carries, in his mouth, his "thorn in the flesh," his shame. He would have much preferred the broken half to remain in place. He wonders, why? Why would the man allow such to be done to him - a little boy, only a little boy? Why?

24

"Bet you can't lie down in the middle of the public road, Hans." That is Gordon laying down the challenge as he, Hans, Ronald, and Rohan are on their way back to school following lunch recess. The little boy does not want to accept the challenge. He is afraid of lying down in the middle of the public road. Not so long-ago Lorna, Ronald's big sister, was struck by a car and killed. In fact, several boys and girls have lost their lives on the public road, having been struck by some speeding automobile.

The little boy knows he is afraid of being hit by a vehicle, but he is even more afraid of being afraid. He does not like being afraid. And so he accepts the dare – not because he is brave. He is a scaredy cat; he is not brave at all. He accepts the dare because he is afraid of being afraid.

The Little Boy From Water Street

Placing his bookbag on the ground beside the road, Hans waits for two vehicles to pass. With no other vehicles in sight either from the north or south, he walks quickly to the middle of the road, lies down briefly on its hot, asphalt surface with arms and legs spread out, then quickly jumps back up and runs towards the side of the road, his heart galloping.

Later that afternoon, the little boy arrives at his apartment. Word about his escapade on the public road has preceded him. The man stands waiting for him at the doorsteps, leather waist belt in hand. At the bottom of the steps, just off to the side, lies the stray dog, Scrap, vigorously licking one of her paws.

25

*H*ans cannot believe his eyes. He is standing with the man in the middle of an amusement park. His first time in an amusement park. Coney Island has arrived in town. It is night, and the many lights are like nothing he has ever seen before. He takes in the spectacle around and above him, mesmerized, especially staring at the brightly lit Ferris wheel spinning high up in the sky. Of all the rides the carousel became his favorite. I hear him giggling and laughing with delight as his horse goes round and round and up and down. For a moment it transports him beyond his world of beatings, and ridicule, and humiliation, and bullying, and fear, into a world beyond his wildest dreams, into a brightly lit, magical world in which his world is briefly forgotten.

26

A stranger shows up at the apartment. The man with the beard and the serious face comes out to meet him. They greet each other warmly.

The little boy, a sheriff, is in the yard about to confront an outlaw in a gunfight. He pauses the scene, listening to the two men talking and laughing. He has never heard the man laugh before or seen him smile.

A few minutes later, the man goes to the side of the apartment, stoops down, stretches his arm under the structure, and retrieves a brindle-coated pup in his hand. Horrified, the little boy watches as the man gives Fury to the stranger. Fury is the last remaining pup from the litter that Scrap had birthed - the one that he had personally named and had designated as his own.

"Daddy! No," the anguished child cries out. The man ignores him and says goodbye to the stranger who then departs with the pup cradled in his arms. The man heads back into the apartment, leaving the little boy devastated, his dream of having his own "Lassie" obliterated.

We see him sitting on a tree stump beside the street disconsolate and distraught, his frail, scarred, olive bronze back exposed to the noonday sun, tears streaming down his face.

"Hansi? Hansi, you okay?" The voice sounds caring, protective, solicitous. It is Griselda's. She lives at the south end of the street. She stoops beside the little boy, placing one hand gently on his shoulder and asks again, "Little Hans, you okay, love?"

To the little boy, Griselda is the most beautiful man on Water Street. He would stare curiously at him, filled with awe whenever he sees her. He cannot comprehend the phenomenon of Griselda nor does he dwell on the contradiction. He simply accepts her freedom to be. He accepts her without judgement. He accepts her man-womanness and incredible beauty without judgement.

"My daddy gave away my little puppy."

"Aww, don't worry, sweetie. I am sure you will get another one," she replies, her arm gently and reassuringly around his shoulders.

The Little Boy From Water Street

27

There is no clear image before me, only a thick, grey fog, behind which is a blackness. And out of the blackness the man's voice…probing, cajoling, but behind the seemingly gentle persuasion there is some other motive.

"Have you ever seen your mother meeting and talking with any other man?"

A pause…

Silence…

And I see the little boy's eyes. Only his eyes appear, only his eyes, breaking through the darkness and the thick, grey fog. Out of the blackness and the thick, grey fog they appear, brown, wide, fearful…

Silence…

A pause…

At this point a sound intrudes itself into the

event - like an overlay of one layer of something upon another layer of something. It is the sound of children reciting the ten Commandments:

"*Honor they father and thy...*"

The sound of the children's voices trails off, and the little boy's eyes again emerge. There is fear in those eyes.

A pause...

Silence...

And then his voice...tremulous and faltering, "Ye...Ye..."

Silence...

A pause...

Fighting back the tears, the little boy stutters, "Ye...Ye...Yes, Daddy."

28

Yes, the little boy did see - in their apartment on one occasion, in the bedroom that he, his two younger siblings, and the man and the woman shared. On the bed on which the woman and the man slept, he saw. Yes, indeed, the little boy did see. He saw Mr. Bromley lying on top of the woman while the man celebrated his birthday with his other friends outside. Yes, the little boy had certainly seen as he barged into the bedroom interrupting the moment and, in that instant, beholding the scene before him, taking in all he saw with those large, brown eyes. Taking it all in without judgement.

29

*I*nstead of bringing relief, the procedure to lance the infected area of the little boy's upper left arm results in further infection of the arm. He lies in bed unable to sleep. The pain is too much to bear. He bites his pillow (now drenched with his tears) to counter the pain which he now feels, a pain that has since become his constant companion. He weeps, longing for a touch, a hug, words of assurance, but neither the man nor the woman seems moved by his tears. He feels alone, all alone.

The words of Mr. KL's song loops in his mind. Sleep and the darkness of sleep eventually show him mercy, offering him temporary relief from the pain.

30

Two separate admissions to the children's hospital did nothing to bring healing for the little boy, neither did a visit to the obeah man nor use of the herbs he prescribed. Desperate for some positive intervention, the woman takes the little boy to the Roman Catholic Cathedral in the city.

The little boy kneels before Saint Peter. Saint Peter's sightless eyes look down upon him with the disconnected, faraway gaze typical of all the icons in the cathedral. In one of his lifeless hands he holds two keys.

"Dear Saint Peter, ah deh in a lat of pain. Please don't leh me feel pain no mo'. It hurt bad bad bad. Please help me, Saint Peter. And ah promise I gan be a good boy from now awn. An' please mek meh mammy and meh daddy stap fightin'. Duh does mek me feel very sad. Thank you very much, Saint Peter. In di name of di Father, an' of di Son, an' of di Holy Spirit, Ahmen."

After praying to Saint Peter, the little boy lights a candle, puts into the money box the 5-cent bit the woman gave him, and leaves the Cathedral with her, his hand in hers and her hand holding his, expectant, hopeful, but still in unbearable pain.

31

*Y*es, indeed, the little boy did see. It is early afternoon. Sunny. The little boy saunters lazily along quiet and dusty Water Street. He is bare-feet and in short, dingy, khaki pants. No shirt, but the old welts and the fresh welts visible on his back, and his torn-up batty pants completely worn out at the backside, exposing butt cheeks. The occasional dray cart passes him in either direction. As he walks along stick in hand and caught up in his own reverie, he absent-mindedly lops off buck beads growing beside the street...

"...like the boy who lops
The thistles' heads,"

The preceding is from Goethe's poem, "Prometheus." Do not ask me how I know. I just know. I know things and have no idea how I know them.

The little boy notices a car up ahead. A woman stands on the driver side. He recognizes her. It is the woman. He draws closer. She does not see him.

A man sits in the driver's seat of the car smiling up at the woman and talking to her. Mr. Clamence!? The woman smiles as the man talks to her. In that instant, the realization of the woman's beauty strikes the little boy. He always knew she was very beautiful, but it was in that instant that the fact fully registered in his mind.

The little boy comes to a halt. He watches, trying to make sense of the situation before him. He has a feeling that the interaction before him contravenes some specific code, but he lays the potential contravention squarely at the feet of the driver of the car. Is that Mr. Clamence? Mr. JeanBaptiste Clamence? Concerning the woman he cast no judgement, neither favoring nor disfavoring, but towards the driver, he feels an anger forming inside him.

The woman sees the little boy and hurriedly leaves off talking with the driver. He, in turn, hastily drives off, passing the child and casting him a brief glance as he drives by. It is Mr. Clamence! It indeed is! Mr. Clamence is one of the village's more affluent inhabitants. He, his wife, and their two teenage children live in a big house on Public Road.

The woman walks towards the little boy, takes him gently by the hand, and together they walk back to Lot 4. The woman talks to the boy as he walks beside her.

"Do not tell your father, okay?"

And again the sound of children's voices interrupting the event. Again that recitation of the ten Commandments, "*Honor...thy mother.*"

The sound evaporates. The little boy lowers his head as he walks next to the woman. And then, after a brief silence, he replies, "Okay, mammy."

Yes. He did see. And more such encounters he observed...at the dark end of Water Street – "At the Dark End of the Street."

They're gonna find us...
Oh, someday...
You and me,...
At the dark end...
Of the street...

32

The city street is abuzz with activity. It is night. Christmas Eve night. The little boy, the man, and the woman are walking along the sidewalk just in front of Rafferty's on Main Street. They are window shopping. The little boy stops at a window displaying a large figure of Father Christmas all decked out in his typical red and white attire. The woman and the man with the serious face continue walking slowly, themselves checking out other displays in the windows. The reddish pink tone of Father Christmas's face alarms the little boy He stands before the showcase studying the figure intently. The costumed figure winks at him. Caught entirely by surprise at this unforgettable occurrence, and super elated at his unbelievable luck, the little boy turns and runs towards the man and the woman, shouting at the top of his voice, "Mammy! Mammy! Father Christmas winked at me! Father Christmas winked at me, Mammy!" Can you hear the excitement in his voice? The realization of his being seen and acknowledged, the realization that he mattered. Just a simple wink, but it means so, so much. It means so much; it means all the world to the little boy.

You might recall that I said you should expect no sentiment from me in relation to the little boy since it is not my place to feel but to simply present his existence events as I receive them. In that regard, you might have seen instances of apparent inconsistency on my part. Well, I am busted. I put up no defense, for I indeed find myself on occasions disposed to feeling for the little fella. Call me inconsistent if you will, but I assure you that I am, for the most part, predisposed to detachment than to its opposite, and I do try as far as is reasonably possible to remain unattached. At times, however, slivers of bias, judgement, and feelings do find their way past my detached aspect. And if my feelings do get the better of me once in a while, let's just chalk it up to my sometimes boredom with the consistent and the predictable.

33

*K*icking and screaming - that action and that sound break forth suddenly and forcefully into the rather subdued atmosphere of a somewhat dark bedroom where began the argument, followed by a loud and fierce fight - another of many such fights between the woman and the man with the angry face. As with every other existent moment there is no color in the image, only black and white, but, in this case, darker gray than white.

In horror, the little boy watches as the fight ensues. It is not a fair fight. One thought that impresses itself on his mind as he witnesses this mismatched (and not too infrequent) episode of brutality was how, despite her being at a tremendous disadvantage, the woman fights back.

The little boy stands helpless as he watches the

violence precipitating on the woman. The banging, the shouting, the man's rage, the look on his face, the wild, jealous hatred in his eyes, the blows he rains down on the woman, her screams, her retaliation with kicks and punches…The little boy watches in fear…in tears…helpless…the pain and sadness he feels at seeing this evolution of violence like a huge boulder in his frail chest. His fragile frame cannot bear the weight of such sadness and inner pain.

The man sits on the edge of the bed holding with his left hand one of the woman's legs (her right leg). Most of her upper body lies under the bed. She kicks with her free leg to ward off the blows the man is raining down upon her. In his right hand he holds a hammer. Yes. You heard me correctly. A hammer. I will say no more at this point; instead, I will leave you with your own thoughts and imagination.

The image of that moment fades quickly, as quickly as it appears. It is an image forever stamped in the little boy's memory. Every time his memory retrieves it, he cringes, seeing the hammer, gritting his teeth, recoiling from the horror of the moment, and quickly drawing the curtains to a close to hide the awful image. But it always returns.

34

*L*et me be clear, I cannot hear in the same manner you hear, for I have no physical mechanism for appropriating sound. My hearing is in my mind.

I hear the words of a song. The voice is that of Ken Lazarus. How do I know? I just know. Intuitively. He sings to a rock steady beat. The song plays in the little boy's mind. I, too, hear it. I hear it because he hears it:

"Tonight," begins each stanza
The first word of every stanza
The singer addresses another
A person unknown, someone alone
In some unknown place
Encouraging recollection while there
Recollection of things learned

There is a feeling of resignation
An expectation of the inevitable
In the very depth of the soul it lies
A certainty of the inevitable
The anticipation of loneliness
An acceptance of loss
Always "Tonight," every night

In some unknown place
Remembering, recalling
Feeling it at the very core
The anticipation of loss
The acceptance of loneliness
Resigning to the inevitable
Every night, always "Tonight"

I hear the words of the song, and I weep inconsolably. In fact, the song produces that same response every time I hear it. But the tears and the sadness are not mine; they belong to Hans. My function is not to feel; I feel no sadness for the little boy. My function is to reflect his existence experience, so if I say I feel sad, the sadness is not mine but the little boy's. But let's not get hung up on semantics. I shall continue with the existence scenario before me.

It is night. The little boy is lying in bed, awake. He cannot sleep. The three other children lie fast asleep on the same bed. Fear consumes the little boy, fear of dying, fear of the dream he dreams each night - an amorphous dream, abstract, without clearly defined shapes or objects. An undulating dream of lines and waves and dark patches with himself caught somewhere in the middle. A recurring dream, recurring each night and recurring in an endless loop in the dream itself. Because of this the little boy dreads falling asleep. And it is that song, "Tonight," that the little boy plays again and again in his young mind to block out the pain, to block out the sadness, to block out the sonorous fear plaguing his mind.

The words of the song make no sense to me or to the little boy whatever its actual meaning or purpose. It is not the words that evoke the overwhelming feeling of sadness and pain, but the song itself without its meaning, whatever that meaning might be. The song is itself mere context, backdrop, with no connection to the emotions evoked in the youngster. It is the little boy's theme song, played in the background of his mind to complement the images of the beatings - the beatings he receives and the beatings the woman receives. It complements the painful event of the broken and subsequently pulled half tooth, the intractable pain resulting from the two abscesses on his upper left arm, and all the other elements that contribute to his fears and pain. It is his night song, his sleep song, his lullaby, his self-soothing mechanism in the absence of the provision of soothing by those responsible for providing that soothing. And so I cry, not because I am sad but because the little boy is sad, not because I am in pain, but because the little boy is in pain, excruciating physical pain.

35

*M*orning has broken. A quiet morning. There is no sound except for the faint humming of the refrigerator and the occasional honking of a motor vehicle.

It is getting gradually brighter outside, with a faint hint of yellow rising up behind the rooflines of the apartment buildings appearing as a blur through the two curtainless windows of the living room. The limbs and branches of a huge tree void of leaves sprawl across the view looking uncannily still, as if stuck there, the foreground of a lifeless landscape.

The room is spacious and bright. A large couch, a large TV, a tall standing mirror, and paintings and photographs on one of the walls are some of the items that adorn the living room. A carpet lies on the floor between the TV and the couch, and a medium-sized Christmas tree stands in the corner of the room, still lit, still draped with decorations, and with a few unopened presents lying underneath.

It is mid-February. February is the coldest month. The room is warm, quite a contrast to the hostile cold outside. A man is sitting on the couch sipping tea, a blanket covering his legs and feet. He feels snug and comfortable. Everything is clear and in sharp focus. He is at peace, in that delightful grey zone, his favorite place of repose, and his world is wonderful and youthful.

Out of nowhere, a song interrupts his thoughts, intruding into his silence without warning. He gets up, retrieves his device from the countertop in the kitchen and returns to the couch. A quick glance in the standing mirror on his way to the couch reveals average height, a full beard partially covering sunken cheeks, sad looking eyes, and an ascetic aspect. Sitting back down on the couch, he searches for the song among his collection of songs. He finds it and presses the play button. As the song plays, he begins to weep, the tears flowing down his cheeks as from some painful place within, but the tears are soothing - cathartic. And the remembrance – the recollection of the unbearable pain in his upper left arm.

A woman comes into the room.

"My love, what's the matter? Is everything alright?" she asks.

The singer's voice fills the room. The man takes a tissue from a packet on the side-table next to the couch. With it he wipes his runny nose.

"I am fine, dear Hozah," he replies. "Just a memory from a time long ago, my dear. I shall be fine."

36

I see nothing before me. There is nothing except that thick, grey fog I sometimes see during these existence moments. Always that same thick, grey fog. And then from the grey thickness, I hear the man's voice - loud, filled with rage and loathing,

"You piece of shit! You little piece of shit!"

Silence.

Then, gradually, from the behind the darkness and through the thick, grey fog, the little boy's face takes shape, his large, brown eyes painfully sad and downcast. And slowly, ever so slowly, that sad little face recedes back into the fog and the blackness, leaving only the fading aura of those large, sad, brown eyes.

37

*H*igh up in the jamoon tree. Yep. There he is. He is in his usual place draped over a branch. That tree which in season offers to him its rich, black, juicy-sweet jamoon fruit. That tree from which, draped on one of its branches, he watches, watching the world go by - his world, the immediate environs of Water Street. Perched on one of its branches, he dreams, escaping the rage, the anger, the brutality, the pain, the shame, the fear. It is that tree from which he employs his imagination, allowing himself to take flight, starring in his own fantasies of chivalry, of rescuing damsels in distress, of leading forth his armies to conquests, venturing into outer space, plumbing the depths of the ocean, defeating monsters and demons and dragons, creating thoughts for the sheep and goats rummaging through the rubbish heap beneath, wondering at the ruminations of the men, the women, and the boys and girls as they make their way to and from the sea-dam, and listening to the winds flowing among the rustling leaves, the birds singing, the insects whispering, and the waves of the Mighty Demerary lapping at its eastern riverbank.

38

*H*ans watches as the man reaches under the apartment and picks up five recently birthed kittens from a shallow depression used by their mother to birth and to feed them. He puts them in a jute bag, secures the mouth of the bag by tying a cord around it, and heads up unpaved Water Street towards the Koker. Puzzled and filled with curiosity, Hans decides to follow the man, doing so at a reasonable distance and pace so as not to be detected. The man turns left past the Koker, heading towards the river. Hans moves in closer. He hears the kittens mewing faintly inside the bag. The man walks across the mud flat past several mangrove trees. He walks to the river's edge and hurls the jute bag with its furry contents into the brown, salty waters of the Demerary. Well hidden behind a mangrove, Little

Hans watches as the man walks back towards the Koker.

And again the sound of children's voices overlies the event. Again that eager recitation of the ten Commandments, the little boy's voice distinct among the children's voices, "...*Thou shalt not kill*..." The voices fade.

He little boy moves from behind the mangrove tree and walks slowly towards the river's edge. The jute bag, now partly submerged, bobs up and down as the muddy brown water moves it upriver. Five kittens. Five drowned kittens. Five dead kittens. Five offerings to Mighty Demerary. Afraid and confused, he hurries back to the apartment, being careful not to be seen coming from the riverbank.

So, I take it that you desire to know. You desire to know outcomes. You desire a working out of things, a redressing, a reckoning, a holding to account. You have an idea of where things might lead. You think you are on to something. You expect things to make sense, to add up. You expect closure. You expect the script to be followed. You expect the sower to reap as convention and the rules dictate. I am afraid I know not how to help you. I cannot help you. I have no answers regarding outcome.

39

$\mathcal{U}$nder the mosquito net covering the bed, the little boy lies awake. Two children younger than he are also on the bed fast asleep. A large sheet hangs from a line in the middle of the room hiding the view of the bed that the woman and the man share and providing them with privacy. Every object in the room is out of focus, collectively presenting an image that looks like an impressionistic painting. Only the sound, the sound in the room and the little boy's thoughts are clear to me.

A steady creaking sound has awakened the little boy out of sleep. The sound is coming from behind the sheet dividing the two sections of the room. It is the rhythmic and repetitive sound resulting from the vertical movement of the bedsprings of the bed behind the hanging sheet.

Along with the repetitive, rhythmic sound, the little boy hears grunts and moaning, the latter coming from the woman and sounding as if she is in both pleasure and pain or one of the two. He does not know for sure which.

This is not the first time that the little boy has been awakened by these sounds. He has heard them before, usually at night. For some unknown reason, he dreads hearing the sounds, and as he has done on the other occasions, he places his pillow over his head to block them out.

As far as he knew, that which was going on in that bed felt out of place with the reality of his experience. He abhorred the thing going on behind that sheet blind. He abhorred its incongruence. He could not understand the emotions it triggered in him – the anger, the hatred, the jealousy, the envy – nor could he understand towards whom his feelings might be directed. He did not know whether to be with angry with the man for that which he was doing to the woman on the bed behind that sheet or whether to be angry with the woman for deriving pleasure from whatever the man was doing to her.

He covers his head with his pillow to block out the sounds coming from behind the sheet blind, but the pillow is ineffective against the importunate sounds.

He bites down on his pillow. He struggles to hold back his tears and to stifle the anger in his chest.

He dreads going to sleep at night. He dreads being awakened by these occurrences of the night. He dreads hearing the sounds. Should he hate the man for whatever he was doing to the woman? Should he be disappointed in the woman? He does not know how to feel nor does he know what to do with his feelings.

Why would he have this passionate feeling of anger or hatred towards the man because of that inscrutable thing going on between him and the woman on their side of the room, but for the beatings both he and the woman have endured at the hands of the man he feels no such disposition towards him. This the little boy cannot understand. He is filled with confusion He cries himself to sleep, quietly.

40

The little boy is awake. He slept well despite the disconcerting event of the night. This moment could be any of those moments that immediately followed the many nocturnal activities he heard between the man and the woman. The moment I describe to you is always the same.

The man and the woman are already up. The little boy gets out of bed and goes into the living room where the man and the woman are sitting and drinking tea. He studies them intently, looking for signs of "last night," for any tell-tale signs of the night's occurrence. He notices nothing.

Shortly after, the man gets up from the table and walks past the little boy. He detects a faint, musky smell emanating from the man. The feeling of anger wells up in him again. Something strange tugs at him from within. He does not understand;

he feels confused. Whatever it was that the man had been doing to the woman, whatever it was that caused her to moan as if she were experiencing pleasure, whatever it was, the little boy detested it. He does not like the man being the source of that pleasure, any man for that matter. Is he jealous of the man? The little boy feels confused; he does not understand.

41

Excitedly, the little boy walks with the man towards the river-dam. They cross a narrow, make-shift bridge connecting the lot to the river-dam, then turn right heading towards the koker. The little boy is filled with eagerness because this will be his first attempt at swimming. He assumes that swimming is simply about the co-ordinated movement of the arms and legs, and he demonstrates to the man (with the movement of his arms) what he would do once he got into the water.

The image shifts. The man is in the water and the little boy is standing on the koker's edge fearful about jumping in. The man comes out of the water, takes his hand (not too gently), and leads him in.

Once in the water, the little boy hangs on to the

man. He is screaming in fear and wishes to get out of the water. The man encourages him to stay calm, but the little boy's is consumed by fear and unable to respond.

He kicks and screams, ingesting the salty water of the Demerary, submerging, emerging, gasping for breath, swallowing water, screaming…

He is now out of the water, desperately trying to get away from the koker. He takes a few steps and falls. He gets up, takes a few steps, and falls again. Darkness. The man comes up behind him and picks him in his arms. It is the only image I have seen of his ever being this close to the little boy. It is a closeness of convenience.

The little boy awakes and finds himself lying naked on the public road and surrounded by voices. Then he is aware of someone lifting him and placing him in the rear seat of a taxicab. He loses consciousness again.

I see him now in the children's ward of the Public Hospital. He stands in the hallway. He knows not what has occurred between the time he was placed in the back of the taxicab and the time of his appearance in the hallway of the children's ward.

He has nothing on but a kaki shirt. The look on his face shows a great deal of anxiety, brought on because of his nakedness and bringing to reality one of his recurring dreams - being naked and surrounded by a crowd of people as they stare at him. He pleads with a nurse who happened to be passing by to help him find his pants. He cannot bear the embarrassment and the humiliation he feels. The kind nurse leads him to a rest room. He sees his pants lying on the floor. He picks them up. Unmindful of the fecal residue lodged in the seam of the pants' backside, he immerses himself into the covering they provided for his nakedness.

42

*G*o ahead. Ask the little boy why he is so often beaten by the man. I bet you he would reply, "Because I am a bad boy." Frankly, I have not seen from him any egregious behavior that would merit the man's brutal response. Like most children, the little boy is at worst forgetful, in possession of a huge imagination, curious, a keen explorer of his surroundings, and always looking for opportunities to play.

He sits on the front steps of the tiny, almost dilapidated apartment. As usual, he is bare-feet, shirtless, and in those torn and dingy khaki pants. Tears are running down his face. He is crying, his thin frame heaving. At various intervals he gasps for breath. His bronze back bears dark welts from the man's leather waist-belt. I see fresh ones there too. The little boy cannot really understand what could occasion such physical violence against him. His can arrive at no other conclusion other than that he is a bad boy.

One thing he always sees in his mind's eyes is the look on the man's face, the look on his face as he administers the beatings. The man's face gives the clue as to the force with which the leather waist belt will come crashing down on the little boy's back. His emphatically determined look. And the hate. Yes, hate. Through the fiery pain the little boy feels and through his screams he can see the hate in the man's eyes

"Hate? But why? What have I done to him to elicit such hatred, such loathing, such brutality?" Those are the little boy's thoughts.

What would you say to him, to the little boy? I know; I know. I have here as elsewhere in my presentation of the little boy's existence moments broken literary convention in addressing you directly. Lay that not to my charge. Take that up with the compositor (used here beyond its denotation). But back to my question. What would you say to the little boy? The truth is, if in fact you did have something to say to him, he cannot hear you. However, you can always find some other little child to whom you can speak your words and to whom your words might be of some comfort.

43

Quite striking about the following segments is that they lack the brevity and the abruptness of the other existence moments I present. They seem more detailed, having the character, not of direct thought or oral transmission, but of literary reflection. They are more artistic in character. These existence segments do not originate in the little boy, nor are they my literary articulation. I know not from what source they are derived. They just are.

Water Street woke up that fateful day to its usual symphony of sounds - a harmonious chorus of kiskadees, roosters, goats, donkeys, cows, and dogs. A fruity, floral aroma filled the dewy air, interspersed with the soft, earthy scent of the rich, green grass and the fresh, salty smell of Mighty Demerary. Still groggy with sleep, the Street yawned and stretched and began the process of slowly releasing its twenty or so families to the new day. And a special day it was. It was the day their nation was about extricate itself from the clutches of its colonial mistress. It was also the day Stefan - rat-faced Stefan - went missing, only to be fished three days later out of the implacable Demerary and thus providing the little boy his own independence of sorts.

For the past weeks the talk of acquiring self-determination could be heard everywhere. And the fact that it was imminent was obvious to all. Posters and flags bearing the colors of the soon-to-be-independent nation were all over the place. And on every radio in every place Mr. Nelson's song could be heard welcoming and celebrating its freedom.

And Water Street's inhabitants, too, became wrapped up in the celebrations, anticipating this most important occasion. And even the little boy and his friends got involved in the festive preparations, though they could not really grasp what all the fuss was about or the significance of the occasion. And since the grown-ups were making such a big deal about it, it was probably important. And while the nation and the village and Water Street welcomed Independence, the little boy and his friends welcomed the fact that there was no school that day. From their point of view, nothing was more important than playing at gun-shooting, climbing trees to get at their delectable fruits, talking about and acting out the "flims" they saw at Mr. Deodat's cinema, and getting into the usual mischief. They considered all the talk about Independence and the related activities trivial and a nuisance, getting in the way of that which was most important to them - play.

44

ater Street is a happy mosaic of ethnicities - East Indians, Blacks, Chinese, Amerindians, and those of mixed descent - all coexisting in relative peace. Water Street was spared the hatred, the acrimony, and the violence that stemmed from racial tensions that existed elsewhere in the nation, especially between the two major ethnicities. It is as if she could care less about the bombings, riots, strikes, demonstrations, and other disturbances that seemed to pervade other parts of the nation. She is too busy nurturing her children, teaching them how to get along with each other and how to care for each other.

Water Street is the western half of a small village lying some six miles south of the nation's capital. Access from the village to the capital and to other villages is via a public road which runs north to south. A notorious section of road it is, having taken the lives of many unsuspecting dogs, cats, and snakes, and the occasional school-child oblivious to the passenger-filled Austin Cambridges, Morris Oxfords, dray-carts, or wooden buses traversing its length. It is in the middle of that same stretch of road that the little boy, around noon one day, had lain spreadeagled in response to a dare by one of his classmates. The word about his foolhardy behavior in the middle of the road that day preceded him to his home, resulting in a sound "cut-tail" from the man.

Houses line both sides of the public road, with a few grocery and cake shops in between, including the Chine'e shop and Bowgie shop, the two most frequented by the villagers. And very often the little boy has been sent to both those shop to deliver a message asking that some item or other be sold to him until the man or the woman got the money to pay for the item. On each of those occasions the little boy carried a heavy load of embarrassment, just like when he often had to tell the rent-lady that the woman was not at home, when, in fact, she was. That kind of relationship with shopkeepers and rent collectors was the rule rather than the exception in the village.

Behind the houses lining both sides of the public road were Hawthorne Street and Water Street - the former to the east and the latter to the west. On the Hawthorne Street side are the back-dam and a huge expanse of sugarcane fields. Water Street runs parallel with voracious Demerary. That lusty river and the cane fields define the little village's character. They are both key sources of village folklore and village livelihood. Most of the men in the village are either fishermen or canecutters, with some of them doing both.

I see you, Water Street,
Adorned with houses on stilts
From which tumble boys and girls
Of all shapes and sizes looking for play.
Girls with braided hair,
And shirtless boys in khaki pants,
Their behinds partly visible
On account of the fabric's wear-and-tear.

I see you, Water Street,
Awash in green trees perpetually offering
Their colorful fruit
And cradling many a young boy,
Lying perched and dreamlike
In the tenuous safety of their branches,
Or sometimes dumping them
Unceremoniously to the ground beneath.

I see you, Water Street,
Awaking at dawn to the cock's crow,
Stirring at the calls of kiskadees,
Guiding the lazy-eyed bovines
Anticipating pastures of sweet grass
As they amble along your unpaved surface
Followed by the occasional donkey cart
Harassed by barking stray dogs.

I see you, Water Street,
Anguished at the news of a passing.
Causing heads to look out of windows,
And bodies to stand in doorways,
Bringing all work to a stop
As the gong sounds its somber, melancholy beat,
Hanging in the air like a dark cloud,
Precedent to announcing the name of the dead.

I see you, Water Street,
At night abetting and aiding illicit rendezvous
Witnessed by restless frogs
Croaking their disapproval
Of the stolen kisses or tender caresses
Exchanged in the darkness at your dark end
Between some woman's husband
And another man's wife.

I see you, Water Street.

The Little Boy From Water Street

45

*O*n this particular day, Independence Day, none of the canecutters sallied forth to the back-dam and to the cane fields. They also had the day off as did everyone else in the nation. In Hans' village the canecutter is special. He cuts an imposing, rugged figure, commanding much respect among the villagers. Bare feet, "black" (from soot), and with his fiery sharp cutlass in hand, he labors in the sweltering heat or in the pouring rain, deftly cutting the sugarcane stalks, tying them together in gigantic bundles, and carrying them on his head and broad shoulders to the punts for transportation to the sugar factory where they are processed into raw sugar and other by-products. They are a band of brothers, these cane-cutters - Black-man, Coolie-man, Dougla-man, their skins blackened by the soot and further darkened by the sun, all working indefatigably together, side by side from sunrise to sunset, getting the job done while working in silence and occupied with their own thoughts, or while talking about cricket, or while simply joking around with one another.

That day, no boat left the Koker to probe the depths of Mighty Demerary or the Atlantic Ocean for fish. The fisherman, too, commands respect in the village. He would depart from the Koker in his motor-powered boat at sunrise, heading out to pens in the middle of salty Demerary or just offshore in the Atlantic, and return at sundown, his boat laden with the catch of fine-shrimps, bangamary, gilbaka, catfish, cuirass, red snapper, and butterfish. The Koker is a hub of activity when the fishermen return in their boats laden with catch. It is the place where adult male and female villagers buy baskets of fish and shrimps from the fishermen to sell in the village or in the other adjoining villages. Some sellers walk around the village with 50lb baskets balanced on their heads while others ride around on their carrier bicycles. Some sellers carry a conch shell which they blow intermittently to announce their arrival, bringing out mothers and housewives to buy shrimp or fish by the handfuls.

While the men are hard at work in their fishing boats and in the cane-fields (or elsewhere), the housewives of the little village are busy with house-cleaning, cooking, grocery shopping, taking care of babies and children, and washing humongous piles of clothes. In between chores they find time to engage their neighbors in mild gossip or in conversations about episodes of "The Guiding Light" or "Portia Faces Life." Occasionally, the gossip might be about some recent death and the related circumstances, or about a wife being beaten by an irate husband on account of that wife's infidelity or some other infraction.

These daily interactions among the women in the village help to alleviate the monotony of their endless chores. And in spite of the seemingly endless work, they still manage to have lunch ready for their husbands and children returning from work and school for their lunchbreak.

46

Water Street's children are its imagination and its innocence. The children provide its energy, its passion. They are its life. They are its narrative and its dreamers. They provide the contrast to the rationality, the skepticism, the ideologies, and the dogma of the grown-ups. Play is their reality; they can't get enough of it. Chores, school, homework, sleep, are all superfluous elements of their existence, totally unnecessary.

Around noon that day, the little boy, as was his custom, lay lazily draped over a branch of the jamoon tree in the backyard of the lot on which his family and four other families lived. He lay perched high up in the tree and as such commanded a view of the rubbish heap below, as well as the sea-dam, the pathway on the side of the lot that led to it, the Demerary, and the nearby houses along the edge of the sea-dam. It was in that jamoon tree that he could often be found if he were not in school or if he were not playing with his friends. The jamoon tree was his sanctuary, his retreat, his hiding place. It was that place from which he watched, that place from which his imagination often takes flight.

A solitary goat rummaged through the rubbish heap looking for any discarded plantain and cassava skins it could find. From the latrine just off to the edge of the rubbish heap, and which served the needs of the families on the two adjoining lots, came the forceful release of stomach gas precedent to the expulsion of fecal matter. It is Meldy, neighbor Rachel's massively overweight daughter who sold black pudding on the side of the street on Fridays and Saturdays and who was the constant object of derision and taunting by several of the children from Water Street.

A few minutes later Meldy emerged out of the latrine, her dress partly stuck between her behind, and ambled her way back to her apartment to take care of Royston, her invalid son. The little boy stifled an emergent giggle as a marabunta buzzed its way across his view. He warily moved his head backwards, keeping his eyes on that dreaded, brown insect and relaxing only when it was safely away from him. The goat continued to paw at the rubbish below, a kiskadee flitted restlessly from branch to branch in the jamoon tree, and the little boy returned to his reverie.

A cry as of someone in pain interrupted the little boy's flight of fantasy. Looking down, he saw Rohan and rat-faced Stefan on the pathway that led to the sea dam. He had not heard them approach, so occupied was he with the story taking shape in my mind. Stefan, laughing, had Rohan in a headlock.

"Yo' hurtin' me!" cried Rohan.

Stefan continued laughing then finally let go. Rohan began to cry, rubbing his teary eyes with the base of his right palm. Stefan slapped him disdainfully at the back of his head and said, "Crybaby."

With a scowl on his face, Stefan turned and ambled along the path towards the sea dam. Rohan rubbed at his eyes once more and proceeded to follow him. For a fleeting moment Hans was sure he saw a steely look of hatred on Rohan's face as he walked behind Stefan. Rohan turned his head for a moment, looked up at the tree, then quickly turned his head away again. Hans wanted to call out to him but changed his mind. He watched them as they crossed the hastily-put-together bridge that spanned the trench bordering the lot and the sea dam. He watched as they walked up the embankment and headed off towards the Koker before settling back in his perch and watching the enfolding of existence.

The little boy was deposited into his world without a script, squeezed out into existence with no template, dumped with no manual, or with no roadmap for being in his world or navigating it. A script was given to him without explanation and with no input expected of him regarding its contents. The contents were entirely non-negotiable; they demanded absolute compliance.

He soon observed the existence of different and competing scripts among adults and that their practices did not always follow the principles enshrined in their various scripts. Moreover, at times, his own sensibilities, feelings, and instincts seemed incongruent with the scripts' requirements, causing in him no small amount of confusion.

And so the little boy is left confused, finding as his only recourse that other world - the world of his imagination, that world in which he retains absolute control, in which play is permissible, a child being a child is permissible - a world bereft of confusion, a world in which he feels safe and in which every child is safe.

47

The familiar sound of an "engine" revving indicated that Gordon was about to make his appearance along the path. He was always driving a vehicle or riding a horse whenever he was on the move. What Hans always found funny were the moments when Gordon had to park his pretend vehicle or dismount and tie his imaginary horse. He would go through the motion of shifting gears and backing up and moving forward or dismounting his horse and tying the reins to an imaginary hitching post. This time he was driving one of those huge tractor-trailers with hydraulic brakes. He brought the truck to a stop, hydraulic brakes hissing and all, and hit the pretend horn (his voice, of course) to get Hans's attention.

"Oi, Hans," he shouted, looking up at Hans in the jamoon tree, "Yo' nah coming wid we?"

"Weh yo' ah guh?"

"To the Koker. Rohan and Ronald are probably there a'ready," Gordon replied.

"I saw Rohan walk by...with Stefan..., but I didn't see Ronald."

"I jus' drove by Ronald's house. He's not at home. He must have walked along Water Street to get there."

Water Street is an unpaved back street. The stones that protrude from its surface are the cause of many stubbed toes. This was, of course, to be expected since almost all the children went around bare-feet. A stubbed toe was one of the most feared experiences of growing up on Water Street. That sudden, unexpected, and forceful contact of big toe with stone, that head-on collision of flesh and stone, the explosion of pain as it makes its way in a flash through one's body, the throbbing of the injured part, and the subsequent soreness, all combine to create one of the most horrifying of childhood experiences on Water Street.

"Bannas, I can't come. You know I'm not allowed to go on the sea-dam or anywhere near the river or koker. I don't want to get into trouble with me Ma," the little boy said.

The man and the woman had forbidden him from going on the sea dam or from swimming in the river or in the koker without a grown-up present.

Kokers are vertical gates that control the flow of water during high or low tide between a major river and canals flowing inland. They can be found along both sides of the river and are usually the launch points for local fishing boats going out for the day's catch.

Unsuccessful in his attempt to get Hans to accompany him to the koker, Gordon varoomed off in his tractor-trailer.

Almost unnoticed, the morning had become overcast, with the sun retreating before the cloudy onslaught. It was an ominous sign that added to the mood for that which was about to unfold. Later that day rat-faced Stefan had been reported missing. The little boy was one of the last persons to have seen him alive.

48

*E*ven the sun was silent that day, giving over its place to a sheet of dark cloud and with the winds beating a gentle, mournful wail. It was as if the very heavens were in mourning. It began to rain - not the usual watery gift that one would expect on an overcast day, but ashes. It was raining ashes, ashes falling like black tears from the sky. On the horizon the black smoke from the burning cane-fields could be seen wafting its way heaven-ward like an offering, adding to the dark, grey gloom that hovered above, offering the promise of rain but instead complementing the sadness emanating from the crowd below.

The little boy thought of the clothes hanging on the clotheslines. At the woman's request, he had not too long hung them out to dry. He thought of them hanging there, vulnerable to the sooty torrent and in need of being washed all over again. But for him and his friends, the ash-like downpour meant a trip to the cane-fields the next day, raiding the punts for the sweet, burnt cane and spending many hours swimming in the warm, muddy-brown canal. But whether they would go to the cane-fields together remained to be seen, for they hadn't seen or spoken to one another since the incident involving Stefan and Rohan. The rumor circulating on Water Street was that Rohan had pushed Stefan into the Koker. Stefan did not know how to swim.

Hans allowed his mind to wander, leaving for a while the somber gathering and thinking of the critters and insects that were wiped out in the fiery conflagration in the cane-fields and thinking of those that managed to escape. He could only imagine what Hell would be like. He wondered whether Stefan were there now, in that place "where the worm does not die and the fire is not quenched." At least that's how Pastor Brimstone had described that dreadful place in one of his sermons at the Assemblies of God church where he attended Sunday school. And where else could rat-faced Stefan be? Certainly not in Heaven - not for his sacrilegious drinking from Father Teufel's chalice or for his bullying of the younger boys of Water Street. He was probably this minute being made to walk across the sharp sword spanning the fiery pit - the ordeal that his friend Unas Khan had told him about. Stefan would never make it across that sword. The little boy shuddered at the thought. He could, but reluctantly, go along with grown-ups being sent to the fiery pit. But children? Sending children there? No! Not even Stefan.

A sudden scream jolted him from his reverie about Stefan's possible final and fiery destination. It was one of Stefan's aunts, wailing and dangling between two other women dressed in black. They struggled to hold her up on her feet while another woman stood by fanning her.

The little boy looked around at the crowd, studying their faces. Everyone had that far-away, contemplative, and almost pitiful look. As usual, neighbor Sybil was there. She was always there, at every funeral, at every wedding, and at every event on Water Street. And she always cried at the funerals. The little boy figured she was probably related to everyone else on Water Street, for why else would she cry? And she was always so dramatic about it, always crying out "Gawd!" or "Jeezas!" in her carryings-on. Was she for real, or was she just putting on a show, he wondered. It was hard to tell.

49

*L*ike the other curious children of Water Street, the little boy, too, was trying to get a look at the body in the open coffin. Funerals scared him, but a sort of sordid curiosity always drew him to them. The thing about funerals that always stayed with him was the smell. It was always the smell - the fruity smell of flowers, but to him the fruity flowers smelled like Death. The smell worked its way up nostrils, clung to clothing, and hung ostentatiously in the air. That day the smell seemed stronger than usual, thicker, sickly sweet, and over-powering. The coffin was of varnished wood with shiny silver handles on the sides, and the usual coffin shape. It was the shape one saw whenever one thought, "coffin." The very word itself conjured up something dreadful. And why did they have to be shaped that way? To the little boy the coffin was the shape of death. He preferred the rectangular, wooden boxes the Muslims living on Water Street used for their funerals, like the one neighbor Roshon was buried in. Those simple, rectangular boxes seemed to make death more palatable. Plus, they were usually covered in white fabric and did not have that morbid, death-like, shiny brown look of the typical coffin, wide at the head and shoulders and tapered at the feet.

Death, the experience of someone's death, that is, left the little boy with a feeling of emptiness, as if something were missing. It was like a pulled tooth - undesirable, painful. It made him anxious. It made him feel vulnerable, especially when the dead was also a child. It underlined the uncertainty of things, underlined the inscrutability of existence, and reiterated that he had no control. It meant that he, too, could be gone at any moment, like Bibi, one of his classmates who died a few weeks earlier, and like Stefan, not that he cared whether Stefan had died or not. In fact, his death brought to the little boy no small amount of relief. It brought emancipation from his bullying.

50

First among the children to get near enough to see Stefan's body was Hans. Shirtless (exposing dark welts on his back, and a few red ones too), bare-feet, and in dingy khaki pants with worn-out backsides showing his butt cheeks, he looked out-of-place among the throng of mourners clad in their black or purple. He squeezed his way through the mourners (mostly women), many of whom wordlessly castigated him with their acidic stares. Once he got close enough, he simply stood there watching, looking down at Stefan's body. He felt a hand on his shoulder. It was Gordon, also bare-feet and shirtless and potbellied. He had made his way through the crowd to stand beside Hans. Neither said a word to the other. What could one say in the presence of Death? And especially, Stefan's death.

Death seemed to have been paying Water Street frequent visits lately. In fact, there is a cemetery at its northern entrance and an old Chinese cemetery at its southern end - two parenthetical enclosures locking in their dead, the inhabitants of Water Street. Someone was always dying, or so it seemed, like neighbor Betty who, one week before, fell dead in her yard in the pouring rain. The little boy remembered seeing her lying there face down in the mud. Some of the neighbors said that she had drunk poison. Strangely, the ingestion of poison seemed to be the preferred method for suicide among the younger East Indian women in the village.

Then there was Lorna, beautiful, long-haired Lorna, Ronald's oldest sister - Lorna on whom the little boy had a crush. She was struck down on the public road by a speeding taxicab, her life snuffed out, her beauty wasted.

Some of the dead were old men and women whose time was certainly up. And of course there was the occasional cat, or dog, or snake run over by an automobile, their bodies left on the road to rot, their carcasses pounded by the elements and by numerous tires, and their stench a constant presence soon to become a mere memory in one's nostrils.

51

But on this day it was the sweet, sickly smell of a plethora of bouquets displayed around Stefan's coffin that filled the air. The coffin lay propped up on a stand in the yard space just off to the side of the little boy's apartment, part of a slightly elevated two-family structure. You could not stand under the building, but it was elevated enough for you stoop down underneath, a nesting place for cats, dogs, chickens, and rodents. Stefan lived with his parents and siblings in the adjoining apartment at the back. The section of the apartment rented by the man and the woman faced Water Street. A small garden, tended by the man, and rich with ochro, bora, and corilla plants, occupied the space between the street and the apartment.

The crowd of mourners had spilled over to the

next lot and onto the unpaved street. The precipitation of ashes from the heavens had ebbed somewhat. Stefan's body, adorned in a white shirt and black tie and black pants, lay in the coffin, sightless, its cloudy eyes staring blankly at the great expanse above. One of the women standing at the foot of the coffin remarked how peaceful he looked. He certainly looked peaceful, too peaceful it seemed, and pure, belying that which the little boy knew about him. The white, ruffled linen that lined the insides of the coffin seemed to give him that purity.

The phenomenon of the open eyes of the lifeless body lying in the coffin perturbed the little boy. Why are its eyes open? Why aren't they closed? He could not shake the questions.

A feeling of fear came over him. He wanted to get away from there, but he could not move. Curiosity riveted him to the spot. One of the mourners reached down and attempted to close Stefan's eyes but without success.

A solitary fly buzzed about the coffin and soon around Stefan's head. His head seemed unusually large. Distracted by the insect, the little boy forgot for a while the sight, the sound, and the smell of Death. He imagined Stefan raising his hand to brush away the annoying fly which was now hovering around his eyelids. The gnat, too, seemed curious about those sightless, staring eyes, but without the questions. It buzzed around a bit more, became tired of peering into those vacant eyes, and proceeded to explore the rest of Stefan's face. It landed first on his nose, then on his lips, seemed to lose interest, and then buzzed off. The dead held no appeal for the restless and easily distracted insect. It flitted away to engage in more rewarding explorations, leaving the living to tend to their dead, to ponder their own existence, to contemplate their place in the larger scheme of things, and to question whether they, in fact, did matter.

52

Someone finally solved the problem of Stefan's recalcitrant eyelids. While the little boy stood beside the coffin daydreaming, one of the mourners, hoping to keep them closed, had placed on the eyelids two discolored looking pennies. Or were they perhaps put there as payment for Stefan's passage across the river Styx? On one of the brown obols the head of the monarch of the mother-country could be barely seen, perhaps worn down from many exchanges.

A few of the women in the crowd began to sing "Abide with Me," and soon everyone started to join in, including the beautiful "Miss" Griselda decked out in a close-fitting purple dress and with a purple veil covering "her" huge afro. That hymn, "Abide With Me," the anthem of many funerals, was the signal that the coffin would soon be covered and Stefan's body be moved to its final resting place. Neighbor Wilhelmina began to wail mournfully, holding her stomach in anguish and crying out, "O, Stefan! Stefan!" After all, he was her son.

The singing continued, picking up in intensity. A few other women, including, of course, neighbor Sybil, joined Stefan's grief-stricken mother. And, as if on cue and in solidarity with the melancholy gathering, a bauxite-laden Saguenay blared an agonized, loud, and mournful moan as it slowly wended its way up the Demerary - Mighty Demerary, bearer of bodies and bearer of ships, bearing also for a few hours in its silty, brown depths the lifeless body of Stefan before depositing it without ceremony on its muddy, eastern riverbank.

53

"Don't let the children cry."
Just listen to him sing.
"Or you're gonna have to tell Alcapone why."

I hear him singing at the top of his voice those two lines.

And then he bursts into, "Don't call me Scarface. My name is Capone. C-A...P-O...N-E, Capone." Placing strong emphasis on the last word.

Just look at him. He appears joyful as he walks blithely along Water Street, seemingly without a care in the world and now stuck on the line, "Don't let the children cry."

The man has not yet returned from work, so the little boy decides to make the most of his extended freedom As usual, he is shirtless, bear-feet, and in his dingy, worn-out-at-the-rear khaki shorts - his butt cheeks exposed. And of course, the welts on his back, old and recent, are clearly visible.

He sees a cluster of buck-bead stalks growing at the side of the street. He stops, picks a handful of the dried beads, puts a few of them in his mouth, and continues on his way.

Looking ahead of him, he observes a familiar figure on a bicycle riding shakily along the street. He stops singing immediately. It is the man. His heart racing, the little boy watches as the man passes him by, a bland look on his face. He is covered in blood. He says nothing as he rides by, blood trickling down his head and face.

The little boy finds out that the man had gotten in a fight with a group of men because of his affiliation with a certain political party that embraced communism. He has no idea what communism is.

The man looks like the men in berets in the photos on the wall of the apartment. He has a beard like those men and sometimes wears a black beret like theirs. The neighbors on Water Street call him, Castro, and they call the little boy, Castro' son.

Quite often, the little boy would see the man standing before the shortwave radio in the living room listening to Radio Havana Cuba. Most of the man's interaction with the little boy involved telling him to do this or do that or beating him with the leather waist-belt. The little boy has no recollection of the man hugging him or playing with him. His best moments at home were when the man was away at work, but his worst moments were those moments when he saw him returning home from work riding his bicycle.

But the little boy gives the man the benefit of the doubt. In his mind he is a bad boy. His syllogistic deduction goes like this: The man does not like me, for I am a bad boy. Since I am a bad boy, he beats me. If I were not a bad boy, he would like me and not beat me. What do you expect a child to know about the principles of logic?

And yet, despite the beatings, he likes the man, for, after all, the man can pass through solid walls. The man is also unafraid of earthquakes. Early one morning the little boy was awakened by powerful tremors - the apartment was shaking violently. He awoke in that instance and saw the man standing calmly and composed as the earth beneath the apartment was heaving. He marveled at the man's fortitude and at his bravery. He wanted to be as brave and as unafraid as he.

But this evening there will be no beating. The man has his own wounds to take care of.

54

*G*iver of life, sustainer of life, and taker of life - that is the Mighty Demerary. In its muddy brown water just near its east bank, the distended, naked body of a man bobs back and forth and up and down - the picture as of a mother rocking her sleeping baby. But this is not the sleep of one living but of one dead, one of many who fell victim to the insatiable appetite of the voracious Demerary.

The little boy, bare-feet and shirtless, his welted bronze back exposed for all to see, stands among the curious crowd of onlookers watching from the muddy riverbank as the naked and disfigured body floats on its back in the water, bent arms pointing upwards as if offering a hug and legs bent at the knees also pointing upwards.

The body reminds the little boy of an animal

roasting on a spit. This is not his first time seeing a dead person, and there is no fear in his young mind as he contemplates the dead, only awe and wonderment as he stares at the body, concluding that death is like a freezing in place, the absolute cessation of motion.

The image of the body in the river quickly fades. Another image replaces it. The two images appear to be contiguous, but that does not mean they are sequential. The boy's existence events as I receive them are never connected by time. They are never presented as before or after, or first, then second. They just are. They are neither connected, nor joined.

The image of the dead body in the river is replaced by another image of the river. In this image the little boy, his friends Rohan, Gordon, and Ronald and some other boys from Water Street are standing at the river's edge playing ducks and drakes.

Several of the boys are considering going for a swim out to a pen in the middle of the river. By this time some grown-ups had shown up, including the man and the fathers of a few of the other boys. They decide to join the boys as well. The little boy had no intention of swimming. Despite being a good swimmer now, he fears swimming in the Demerary especially since it almost took his life. He prefers swimming in the canals near the sugarcane fields. But when the man indicated that he, too, was going to join the group for the swim, the little boy immediately discarded his fear and decided to join in. In his mind, he saw himself and the man, son and father, swimming together out to the pen and back, and thought that nothing could happen to him if he were with his daddy. And more importantly, this was an excellent opportunity for him to impress the man with his swimming ability as the man has never seen him swim since had he learned to do so following his near fatal experience in the koker.

The boys all undress completely. The men keep their shorts on. Then everyone plunges into the muddy brown, salty water. The little boy keeps his eyes on the man and quickly positions himself to be side by side with him as the water flows moderately up-river.

Not too long after, the little boy notices the man pulling away from him. He increases his strokes to catch up but to no avail. The man increases the distance between them.

The little boy panics and cries out, "Daddy! Daddy! Wait for me!"

The man maintains his pace, giving no indication whether he has heard the little boy who by this time has started to cry. He contemplates turning back but adjudges that he had proceeded too far into the swim to do so and decides to continue swimming to the pen.

The little boy realizes that he is in a dangerous situation. He is all by himself in the Mighty Demerary - the taker of many lives. The others in the group are way ahead and almost at the pen. Still crying, he keeps on swimming, refusing to give up, utilizing all his skills, willing himself forward, for he must show the man that he is capable. He must prove himself. He had pictured himself and the man swimming together - one filled with pride, the other, the source of that pride. But alone, he reaches his goal. Alone, he arrives at the pen. But just as his hand touches the boat moored at the pen, those already in the boat begin plunging into the water for the swim back. The little boy is extremely shocked, but he figures that the return would be easier than the out swim.

And so, alone, and filled with disappointment, he swims back towards the starting point, the Mighty Demerary showing him mercy and kindness and depositing him on its muddy, eastern riverbank safely.

55

"My name is Bede Moses," answered the boy from the Interior Savannah. And thus began the friendship between the little boy and his Amerindian friend, Bede - a friendship, real or imagined, that lasts for two weeks, following which the little boy never sees his friend again.

The two friends are hospitalized, each on account of a problem with one of his arms - the little boy, on account of two abscesses on his upper left arm and Bede, on account of a broken left arm. I have no details of those two weeks. No other image emerges except for the following: I see the Amerindian boy - his childlike face, his black hair, his perfectly formed teeth, and his blue shirt and khaki pants. I see the sadness on the little boy's face when he wakes up one morning to find his friend gone, and I also see his look of consternation when the nurses, in response to his query as to his friend's whereabouts, said that they did not know any patient named Bede Moses.

Is Bede real? Is he merely a figment of the little boy's imagination? But why should that even be a question? The little boy does not give priority to the world of sense experience over the world of imagination, designating the former as real and the latter as unreal. For him the world of his imagination (readily intelligible and accessible and in which everything is possible and permissible) is the real world, Plato, Kant, Hegel, and others be damned.

I see Bede. I hear his voice. I hear his voice saying, "My name is Bede." I hear the manner in which he says it. I hear the words of the song he teaches the little boy during those two weeks. I hear in my mind that song - the song about the Rupununi, about its big bright stars at night, its wide, high savannah skies, and its sweet, perfumed trees in bloom. I do not know why I see him and the nurses do not. All I know is that I see him just as the boy sees him. Does that that mean I am the boy? I know you would ask that question. No. I am not the boy. I am merely the custodian of his existence moments – nothing more.

The little boy's existence moment with his Amerindian friend from the Rupununi cannot be expressed in prose narrative. Prose narrative cannot effectively represent it or effectively capture its meaning and significance. The details are not clear. The details are there, but they are subsumed in the dark depths of memory or visual recollection. They are there; they are not lost. They are there, but gently and securely submerged in feeling - in the little boy's feelings.

And so I struggle to express in prose narrative the little boy's experience of his Amerindian friend. It can be effectively expressed only poetically, just as, according to Johannes Climacus, Mozart's *Don Giovanni* can be expressed only musically, not in language. And so, likewise, I am here constrained to rely on the poet, Sabio, to express poetically the little boy's experience of Bede. No, I have no information on Sabio. Anyway, listen as Sabio recites the ballad of these two young friends.

Amidst the smell of the dead
And while lying on a hospital bed,
We sang of the big, bright,
Night stars of the Rupununi,
Of its wide, high savannah sky,
And its sweet-perfumed, blooming trees.
It was the song he taught me,
And to this day still lovingly remembered.

"My name is Bede," he said,
With diction amazingly perfect.
Bede, my friend for one week,
Perhaps my best friend ever,
With eyes of huge black pearls
Complementing an innocent face -
A hint of sadness lying beneath.
Out in the rain we play,
Calloused feet in soft, muddy clay.
Climbing mango trees
And chasing cows with sticks,
Harassing dogs stuck in copulation.
And pelting stones on rooftops.
Two shirtless waifs with smooth skin
Darkened by Apollo's element,
Laughing and frolicking in a happy world.

But this was what I dreamed of,
What I hoped would be.
Our real world was the Ward,
That place for the innocent, young infirm,
That place from which many did not return,
From which Bede never returned,
O Bede, come out from your hiding.
Where are you, Bede?

We were Conquerors in that Ward,
Among bedpans and the bandaged,
Hailing porters pushing gurneys,
Counting the emerging symbols
Of our imminent manhood,
And falling in love
With our white-capped,

White-aproned goddesses.
Big-eyed Bede,
Alive and of this world
When I last saw him,
Or so I thought.
He, of whom I conversed not,
About whom I said nothing,
And with whom no one spoke but I.

Bede, in light-blue shirt and khaki pants,
The only one not in pajamas,
But that which, at the time,
I didn't think unusual.
He wasn't there before,
And then one night, unexpectedly,
He was there,
At first to my extreme fright,
But eventually to my utmost delight.
Numerous were the strange
And curious looks we received -
Or at least I received -
As we ran screaming delightfully
Around the sterile Ward,
Oblivious to the mutterings
Of the bed-ridden
Or the displeasure of our goddesses.
O lonely the night when he was there
As we played under the white sheet
And then suddenly there no more.
The white-capped goddesses
No answer could give
Concerning my plaintive inquiry,
Ardently denying any knowledge

The Little Boy From Water Street

Of my indigenous friend.

"Who is this Bede?" they asked.
O, Bede, come out from your hiding.
Where are you, Bede?

Childhood to adulthood
Will at some time capitulate,
And play, of necessity,
By toil be replaced.
Flowers will fade,
Landscapes will change,
Hair once abundant
Will recede in a mass of grey,
And from my own loins
Might sprung forth those
Destined to carry on my name.
But Bede will remain the same.
Bede in his short, khaki pants
And light-blue shirt,
Sad-eyed and innocent,
Bede, unchanged,
Wearing that childlike face still.
Unexpectedly reunited we shall be,
Though long separated
By a world distant, yet near,
Opaque, yet accessible,
But for now only to a few.
Reunited – and regularly blessed
By his oft unexpected visitations –

Bede, once my friend for a week,
Soon my Guardian and Guide to be,

But my friend in a life long past,
Or so I was told -
Our story yet to be played out
In this drama of existence.
And our connection
To be no longer by play defined,
But by some higher purpose.
And in the years hence
When a man I shall become,
I shall dream of that time,
Of that week years past when...
Out in the rain we could have played,
Calloused feet in soft, muddy clay.
Climbing mango trees
And chasing cows with sticks,
Harassing dogs stuck in copulation
And pelting stones on rooftops.
Two shirtless waifs with smooth skin
Darkened by Apollo's element,
Laughing and frolicking in a youthful world

The Little Boy From Water Street

56

"No! There is no god. I am God." Those words are all I hear, loud words coming from the darkness and from behind the thick, grey fog. They are the man's words, words he spoke in response to the little boy who had excitedly told him how he had prayed to God and to Saint Peter, asking them to heal his upper left arm.

Those words still hang in the air. They hang there frozen, like an absurdity.

Silence.

I see nothing before me. I see nothing except that thick, grey fog, that same thick, grey fog behind which lies blackness, a darkness.

Silence.

Then, gradually, from the behind the darkness and through the thick, grey fog, the little boy's face takes shape, his eyes welling up with tears,

tears of sadness, tears of confusion.

No God?

No "In the name of the Father and of the Son and of the Holy Spirit...Amen."?

No "Gentle Jesus meek and mild, look upon this little child."?

No "Holy Mary Mother of God" to pray for this sinner, now...to pray for this little boy?

No absolution from Father Teufel?

No Shiva? No Krishna? No Vishnu? No Kali? No Ganesha? No Lakshmi? No beautiful stories of Kunti, Arjuna, Karna, Bishma, Duryodhana and others from the Mahabharata?

No Allah to give meat or coins to the poor? No prophet Mohammed (peace be upon him)?

No God?

With the tears streaming down, the little boy remembers the time the man had also said that there was no Father Christmas - that he was Father Christmas and that the family did not need toys but that they needed food on the table and that since he was the one putting food on the table, he was Father Christmas.

It was Christmas Eve, and the little boy had expectations of receiving toys just as he had the previous Christmas. He could not grasp the idea of Christmas without toys. No toys!?

The woman had stood there just watching and

listening as the man carried on. Without saying a word, she changed her clothes and left the apartment.

The little boy sits at the doorsteps of the apartment unable to make sense of that which the man had spoken earlier. No God? His world has been irrevocably thrown into chaos. Sunday School, bible class, serving as an altar boy at Saint Peter and Saint Paul's Church, attending Maktab at the village Mosque, and listening to the stories from the Mahabharata at the Hindu Temple on Water Street have lost all relevance and significance. He hoped for a miracle such as the one that occurred that past Christmas Eve. He remembers the woman - Veronica, his mother. He remembers her returning after she had left without saying a word that Christmas Eve. She had returned later with two bags in her hands. She had salvaged his Christmas. The two bags were full of toys. But now, this? No God? No healing of his upper left arm? No miraculous removal of the pain? The despair in the little boy's eyes is obvious. Slowly, very slowly, he feels his world disintegrating around him. Who will salvage God for him? Who will give God relevance again? Who will give back God to him? Who will make his world right?

57

*C*an you imagine the fear? Can you imagine the weight of this moment. Can you imagine the overwhelming burden of this moment?

I watch as Nathaniel, a wooden truncheon in his hand, rains blow upon blow upon blow on his defenseless wife. With tears streaming down his face, Hans Kindermann watches too. Fear fills his very soul. He finds himself standing face to face with the Universe. He must make a decision. Does he dare step outside the Universal? Does he "dare disturb the Universe"...and in doing so effectively upend it? He makes his decision.

"Daddy! Daddy! No!"

Yelling those words, the little boy jumps onto the man's back, wraps his left arm around his neck, and, with all his strength, grabs the short, wooden truncheon in the man's right hand. Little

Hans Kindermann hangs on to his father's neck for his mother's sake. He commits himself to his decision and action. He will not let go.

In that moment the little boy had done that which the man had a responsibility to do but did not and could not do. In that very moment little Hans Kindermann stepped outside the Universal. He stepped in as protector. He, a child, became man, the true man. He stepped into the role of protector. He protected his mother from the man whose responsibility it was to cover her, to protect her. In that moment, the little boy stood up to his father. He stood up to God.

From this point forward no one can induce fear in the little Prometheus, no one, not even God. He respects God and acknowledges his matchless power, but now he no longer fears him. He has stood up to God. God has shown himself vulnerable, and because the little boy has seen his vulnerability, in his shame he resorts to revenge, to violence. The leather waist-belt continues to be the mechanism of revenge and the display of power, and while it causes pain, in the little boy there is no fear of the bringer of pain, and neither is there hatred of or anger towards the bringer of pain.

58

*V*eronica and her son Hans Kindermann are sitting in the cinema. They are the only ones I see in the surrounding darkness. I might have said this before but allow me to say it again: The cinema is the place that allows Veronica to escape, and every time she goes there, she takes Hans with her. Cinema soon becomes his paradise and his escape too. It is one of the gifts she imparted to him - love of cinema.

The film's theme song is playing in the background of a scene. Hans cannot comprehend the film, but the song, the voice, evokes a deep sadness in him. The voice is a woman's, melancholic, soothing, wistful, desperate, singing of feeling insecure and lost, of wanting to "get off of this merry-go-round," questioning whether it is all "a dream," and "wondering why, wondering why."

Hans turns his head and looks at his mother.

"How beautiful she is," he muses, filled with love for her - his mother, his Veronica.

Veronica is fully caught up in that which unfolds on the screen. Hans feels sadness for her, sadness for himself, connecting with a song which lyrics he does not understand, a song that plays in the background of Veronica's life, of his own life. For a moment his mind runs on his father. He is uncertain how to feel about him. There is an ambivalence. He remembers that day not so long ago when he dared to do the unthinkable, jumping on his father's back to stop his brutal blows and to protect his mother. In that moment he grasped the significance of motherhood, of the sacredness of a mother, his mother – of motherhood as *a priori*, the first principle of existence, the first principle in the Universe.

Hans turns his eyes back to the screen. He reaches out his hand and takes his mother's hand in his, his heart full of love for her. They simultaneously turn their heads and look at each other, her eyes soft with sorrow. She smiles, her smile breaking through all her sadness and pain. He smiles back at her, finding indeed, in that moment, the world to be *"wonderful and [beautiful], after all."*

59

Residing with the woman and the serious-faced man at Lot 4, Water Street is a little boy, a good little boy. His name is Hans Kindermann. All he wants is to do is play, to plumb the depths of his curiosity and his imagination, to explore the world around him, to observe humanity without judgement. He is always in my thoughts, ever present, though vaguely, like a shadow. I do not know or understand my connection to little Hans or his relation to me or why I am the custodian of his thoughts and memory. He is timeless. He is always a little boy; that means he is neither past nor present. I see him, but vaguely. I know the little boy and yet I do not know him. He is ever present and yet not present. He is both being and nothingness.

Understand this. The little boy is not the one

in need of healing. The children are not the ones in need of healing. They are not the ones who need to be hugged, to be loved, to feel safe. They have endured much, and yet they stand. Damaged, yes, but still they stand. They have withstood much, exceedingly far more than we can ever imagine. Yet they stand fast, holding no grudges, holding no malice. They feel anger towards no one. They feel hatred towards no one. They do not need your, my pity.

It is not you who needs healing, little one. You are not the one who needs to be cried over, to be pitied, to be hugged, to be loved, to feel safe. We adults are ones who are needy. We adults are the ones in need of pity, in need of being cried over, in need of feeling safe, in need of feeling loved, in need of being hugged, in need of healing.

So what then, little one? As custodian of these vignettes of your existence, I offer your vulnerability. I offer your innocence. I offer the healing power of your childhood. I offer the healing power of your story.

POSTSCRIPT

*H*ans Kindermann is his mother's child, the child of the beautiful Veronica. She and he are inextricably linked. She gave him her passion for cinema. She gave him her love of reading. She gave him her quest for love, futile quest though it is. He knows her; he understands her. He understands her quest; he does not judge her.

Some wise person once said, "We seek an explanation for everything, but explainability is not an absolute necessity of phenomenon, whether in regard to the ontological or the teleological." That person also said, "Any occurrence that cannot be corroborated is fiction." So what do those observations have to do with that which follows? I have no explanation. But here is a strange thing. I know, and I know not that I know or how I know, or why I know. However, I suspect you might have some question about the existence event that occurs in the bedroom of the apartment as the man is celebrating his birthday outside. The following, I hope, offers at least some bit of clarity on that event. And as to why I even present it here, I truly have no idea:

"A Reflection" by [a certain] Mr. Bromley, Esq.

"The artist lives in an absurd world that he himself has created to flexibly adapt to his imagination."
                                                    Samuel Mann

 I heard she died recently, the news, an unwelcome interruption of a quiet Sunday afternoon's tea. An annoying encumbrance, to say the least, amidst vaporous and random thoughts setting the stage for rude disturbances of the past like a whimsical rearrangement of superfluities.
 Briefly forgotten was the aroma of pleasantries, the unexpected tidings having suppressed the delectable smell of toasted muffins and expelled the sweet odor of fine tobacco.
 Until now, a distant memory she had remained - my delightful 'Callisto,' long since passed over, with only rare intrusions into my thoughts, bringing about a chuckle or a wry smile.
 Dispassionate remembrances, as I call them, of

a deed long accomplished and forgotten, stripped of guilt and relegated to mere conquest, and, except for those large, brown eyes, without the lingering weight of remorse or regret.

A festive event it was, celebrating Nathaniel's birthday, bringing friends together - friends, friends of friends, and children of friends.

And there she sat, the contumacious host, to me, now, nothing but an amorphous blur, for that was a long time ago when we once were beautiful and youthful, when she was youthful and beautiful.

Amidst conversations about non-essentials and talks about this and about that, she flitted, attending that day to us, her guests, her friends.

And so went the whispered conversation (as I recall) when by design I caught her alone...

"Your words move me, but that which you ask I cannot do, for Nathaniel is my one true love, and your Charisa is my dearest friend. In the eyes of the Almighty this is wrong. How can we do this and sin against God?"

Thus began the siege, as I remember it, precursor to the sustained assault as liquor gave birth to laughter and ignited boldness...and lust...., for my eyes were on the intractable host while her beloved and our friends merrily preoccupied and none the wiser to my scheme, long before hatched, remained oblivious to my amorous overtures.

And so the spirits flowed and so too the lust, my lust by artful and discreet advances masked, but the uncooperative host, like a fortress, remained impervious, rebuffing my eloquent onslaught.

Under cover of the inebriating merriment, to the sacred room I followed her. Unsuspecting she was and worn down by my advances. And worn out from playing host, she repaired to the bedroom and sought brief respite on the sacred bed.

There she lay - beautiful Veronica - her eyes closed, lips slightly parted, beautiful and unsullied despite giving birth. She lay there far removed from the oldness, the oldness that soon catches up with humanity - the oldness that eventually caught up with me, and with her too I suppose, but now mercifully removed from it.

I watched her, banishing reason and embracing passion as on the altar of oblation and copulation she lay. Then, seizing the moment...and at that point, since *"all my arts were vain, I offered force."*

And as I sit here thinking of the dead, it is not on that moment's pleasure that I muse, but on that which keeps coming back to me - those large, questioning eyes, those innocent, brown eyes of the little lad, the shirtless little boy who barged into that fateful room, beholding, and least expecting that tragic scene of friendship's desecration. Those eyes that, in that moment seemed at first confused then subsequently curious, expressing no surprise, and making no judgment.

And after what seemed an eternity, as I recall, the little boy lowered his head and beat a hasty retreat, the dark welts clearly obvious on his frail, bronze back.

The incident in that bedroom and on that bed has long since been forgotten, and fortunately without undesirable outcome, at least for me,... but those eyes...

And..., aah!...there...The smell of muffins, freshly baked, and cinnamon tea's delightfully soothing aroma, and the sweet smell of tobacco...again.

www.ingramcontent.com/pod-product-compliance
Lightning Source LLC
Chambersburg PA
CBHW030303130626
46549CB00002B/678